APHRODITE & HEPHAESTUS

BESTSELLING AUTHOR
Natasha Luxe

Also by Natasha Luxe

Celebrity Crush Series
PLOT TWIST
OFF CAMERA

Club Reverie Series
FAE PRINCE
VILLAIN GOD

The *Heroes and Villains* Series with Liza Penn:
NEMESIS
ALTER EGO
SECRET SANCTUM
MAGICIAN
THUNDER
GODDESS

Never miss a sexy release!
Join my mailing list:
https://rarebooks.substack.com/welcome

1

Aphrodite

The first thing I knew was a rush of light.

Shimmers and pulses came to me, and names to go with them—*peach. Blush. Crimson. Azure.* Colors for the light, shifting in a chromatic wave that ebbed and rose and ebbed again.

And then I was standing on a shoreline, a froth of seafoam glittering down my body, dozens of tiny bubbles kissing my skin as they popped. My eyes parted, and I blinked in the insistent rays of dawn.

In front of me stood—waited—half a dozen beings.

I didn't have the name yet for the way they stared at me. The pulses of light fogged my vision, colors still dancing across my eyes; but I knew they watched me, something primal in them as their gazes dragged down my foam-dressed body, and I named the places as I felt the sensation of their looks.

Chin. Throat. Shoulder.

Breast. Nipple.

Stomach. Navel.

Thigh, one, then another. Knees. Calves.

And then another word—*nakedness.*

I shivered, though the air was velvety warm, and the sight behind these beings yanked my attention.

A beach spread around us, blocked by sharp white cliffs that were marbled with black stone in creeping vines that climbed and climbed and fought for height with the sky. My neck craned; I looked higher, to the left, and saw a mountain, sharply peaked and endlessly tall, stabbing right through that sky, into fluffy white clouds.

Beauty.

When that word rang through me, I clung to it. It burrowed deep into me, to the very root, where it settled and began to blossom, stretching out until I couldn't tell where the word ended and my own skin began.

The cliffs were jagged and harsh, cold and domineering, but that presence held a stately beauty of its own. And the mountain—towering, impassable, wicked.

Beauty. Love.

This is my purpose.

Tears pricked my eyes at the exquisiteness of it all.

"What is this place?" was my first question.

One of the beings stepped forward. My focus drew back to him—I knew it was a him. Knowledge was coming to me faster now, the way waves licked at my heels, and as he closed the space between us, those same waves sloshing around his sandaled feet, I knew the name now for the look in his eyes, the same look the other beings still directed at me.

Hunger.

It made the fizzy sensations on my skin turn tight and uncomfortable.

The being held out his hand to me. "Welcome, Goddess, to

2

Olympus. I am Ares, God of War. Who do we have the pleasure of welcoming into our home?"

Goddess.

Yes, that was right.

"Goddess," I repeated, savoring the word, the roll of it, heft and importance. It gave me power of some sort. Power to do what? "Beauty," I added. "Goddess of Beauty and Love."

Ares grinned. His skin was hewn to gold in the sun, tanned from excessive time outdoors, and when he smiled, it widened his whole face, up into his sparkling eyes, in a way that had the apex of my thighs clenching unwittingly.

Attraction. Sexual.

He had that look of hunger still, and he dropped his gaze down my body again.

"Your name, Beauty?" he asked.

No, do not call me that; I am the Goddess *of Beauty,* I wanted to say, for it felt like an important distinction.

But his eyes were on my bare chest. And I felt that other word again, *nakedness*, and I realized those beings all wore elaborate togas or gowns or tunics, gold-edged and beaded and intricate, while I was entirely nude.

I folded my arms over my chest, pressing my round breasts together, the heat between my legs surging up through the rest of me and souring into shame.

Ares continued to stare. To smile.

His eyes lifted back to mine.

"Aphrodite," I said with force. "My name is Aphrodite."

2

Hephaestus

I watched a handful of the other gods, some my siblings, gather on the beach, my face ducked out of sight in the narrow slit of my forge's window, low at the base of the mountain.

I watched.

Lingered.

The heat of my forge grew at my back—I had left it unattended too long.

But something kept me pinned there. I had seen divine creation before, of course; why did this one keep me irreparably in place?

I knew.

I knew when I saw *her*.

She rose from the waves in an eruption of teal seafoam set to diamond glitters by the sun, and every divine creation I had seen before shriveled and rotted in comparison to this one. This was not a creation. It was a rip in space, and she had been guided through, perfection incarnate sent to be the single point around which our universe would rotate.

Around which *my* universe would rotate.

I felt that tug immediately, a righting of my soul, or whatever soul a god like me had left. *There. She is the one. This is your purpose.*

I shook the thought away, self-loathing crashing through me. My purpose? No—*here* was my purpose, this forge, the bang and spark of my craft, sculpting enchanted armor and weapons and mighty tools that the other gods wielded to bring judgment to mortals.

Ares approached her first.

Of course he would.

She was stunning, her curves round and soft, her eyes bright even from as far away as I was. She had been looking up, at the top of Olympus, but when Ares drew up close to her—too close; my hand fisted on the edge of the stone-cut window—she looked at him.

And recoiled.

My fist clenched tighter. The stone cracked.

I could not hear what he said to her. I could see her lips move, though, the slight tremble to her. If I could see her discomfort around him, then surely all of the gods and goddesses on the beach saw, too. Ares would be oblivious, but not Hera, not Artemis—

Ares took her arm in his muscular fingers and my own bore down so harshly on the window edge that a chunk of stone came off in my palm.

She went with him, stepping out of the sea that had created her, her arms now clamped tightly across her bare chest.

They were staring at her body.

I was staring at her body.

But I caught myself, swallowed hard, willed my stiffening

5

cock to fuck right off. What was she the goddess of, that she demanded this kind of fascination? I watched the others as they turned to follow her and Ares back up the steps, and they were all flushed, eyes wide, tongues darting out to lick their lips.

I turned from the window as they ducked out of sight. My forge raged, flames licking the rocks it was set in, and I rushed to cool it, the iron boots on my feet clanking with each step. As the embers hissed and smoke billowed, sweat poured down my face, lapping at my bare chest, failing to cool the intensity of the heat deep in me.

What I had seen in the others was more than the normal obsession that came with something new at Olympus. I felt it, too, but I hated that I had them to thank for my self-awareness. It allowed me to breathe deeply, nostrils flaring, fighting for calm against the memory of her body sheened and brilliant in the sun, the look in her eyes as she'd stared up at Olympus, innocent wonder and awe.

We were ageless, eternal. *New* was set upon in a ravenous tear until the only thing that remained was a shell, used and sucked of anything that had once made it good and glorious.

So *her*?

She would be hollowed out into one of us by nightfall. And then she would be another body standing at another divine creation, waiting for something, *anything*, to break the monotony of our endless existences.

I lifted my hammer and returned to the project that awaited me. More bolts for Zeus.

But as I raised my tool over a rod of pure, blinding light on my anvil, I saw *her*. Her face, staring up at me, that look of innocent wonder.

The others would destroy her.
Would I just let them?

3

Aphrodite

I was taken up grand marble steps that curved around and around, lifting us up the side of the mountain. Olympus. "Your home now," Ares told me.

The higher we went, the more the wind buffeted us, making goosebumps prick along my arms and harden my nipples. I kept my arms crossed over myself, but I felt the nakedness through every part of me, the way the other beings—gods and goddesses, I realized—were behind me, staring up at the slit between my thighs as I stepped alongside Ares.

He kept his hand on the small of my back. Kept his other hand on my upper arm, his fingers curved in alongside my breast. I did not want him touching me, but I could not yet figure out what was *normal* and what was *unusual* and I knew nothing about this place. Every passing moment brought more clarity to my mind, but I still felt like a lump of clay, a statue before it was baked, soft and malleable.

They saw me as that, too.

We entered directly into the mountain, and a maze of hallways unfolded. Though it was within the belly of Olympus, each hall and the rooms we passed were lit with unnatural white light, highlighting the sheer opulence in every corner. Gold and ivory and silver, jewels and coins and silk; trays piled with food that gave off the most luscious scents, savory and sweet. Sheer curtains hung over doorways, billowing in enchanted wind, brushing the edge of my body as we passed.

The beauty, the luxury, the feel of the fabric lapping at my skin—I shivered.

Ares felt it. His grip tightened on my arm, his thumb gliding over the mound of my breast.

The others behind him drew closer, and I caught a look he shared with one, a woman.

"Get her some clothes, Ares," she said, a coy smile.

His grip tightened. It was almost painful now, the barest hint of it. "Of course, Artemis." His eyes dipped to me. "There is a wedding tonight—you are just in time. We will have you gowned and fashioned to outshine the bride."

The others laughed, high, trilling sounds that made me flinch.

"That isn't necessary—" I started to say, but Ares released me, finally, and I rubbed at the spot his hand left on my arm, lingering heat and a slight swell of pain.

He hailed someone standing up the hall, at the base of a set of wide steps. "You! Come. Care for our new goddess—the Goddess of Beauty and Love. I want her ready and regaled as such by nightfall."

He wanted me ready?

Did I belong to him?

No. I felt the refusal deep in my stomach, thudding against the shame he brought out when he looked at me, the discomfort of all the eyes still on my body.

No. I was the Goddess of Beauty and Love.

I did not belong to anyone.

A trio of young women rushed forward. Their cheeks flushed red as they drew closer to Ares, his towering height dominating them instantly.

"Yes, God Ares, yes," one said, heads bowed in deference, and they surrounded me.

I let these women pull me away as the group that had watched my creation funneled up a staircase. They all stared at me until the hallway parted us, and finally, out from under their gaze, I wilted.

"How may we address you, my lady?" one of the women asked.

"Aphrodite," I said, and when I looked at her, she kept her head down.

"Goddess Aphrodite," she repeated. "Welcome to Olympus—"

"Who are you?"

The three of them noticeably stiffened. They shared a look.

"You do not need to worry over that, Goddess Aphrodite," one said. A different one, with dark hair twisted tight to her scalp. "We are nymphs bound to serve you. Call for aid, and we will be there."

"Do you not have names?"

Again, that look between them. "We do. But, Goddess—"

"Then I will know your names. You know mine."

I saw them all smile. The redness to their cheeks now rose again, this time in joy, and they all looked up at me for the first time.

"Aglaea."

"Euphrosyne."

"Thalia."

I grinned. "Your names are beautiful."

Their blushes deepened. "Thank you, my lady," said Euphrosyne, the one with twisted black hair.

"Come." Aglaea waved her arm to a room we approached. "We will ready you. I can't believe they didn't bring clothes down for you!"

Thalia rolled her eyes. Something had changed in their attitudes—they were no longer meek, and I felt a well of camaraderie, the first true link of connection that was not manipulative.

"Oh, Hera had clothes; didn't you see? She kept them behind her back," Thalia said.

Aglaea shut the door behind us as we entered the room. Her gasp gave noise to the feeling that bubbled in my stomach—confused shock.

They had had clothes for me?

They had kept me naked.

"Don't worry, Goddess," Euphrosyne said. She read the horror on my face. "You are here now, and we will take care of you. Look! What would you like to wear?"

I let them dress me in a long, rippling gown of deepest scarlet, the top nothing more than two lengths of fabric that covered my breasts and connected to a belt of braided gold around my hips. They styled my dark hair, drying and curling it so it fell in soft ringlets around my shoulders, and they brushed my face with rouge and stain and kohl.

I watched them work in a mirror, for the first time seeing what the other gods had witnessed emerge from the waves. *Me.*

I knew beauty. It was imbedded in me, and it called out the way I had heard seagulls crying at the beach. It drew my focus to Euphrosyne's lovely wide nose, and her full lips, and how her left eye was slightly larger than her right, an imperfection that set her whole face to glowing with the way she looked perpetually contemplative. I saw a mark on Thalia's jaw, a scar, and it gave her whole bearing a roughened air that made her fierce. And Aglaea was tall and lanky and while the other nymphs made a joke about her clumsiness, I saw in her the way branches jerked and moved in a storm—how did I have these memories? And yet that was the image that came as she flitted about the room, her long limbs snapping and bowing and holding strong against an invisible force.

And when I looked at my own face, I saw the long point of my nose, the deep golden brown of my skin, the plump rose of my lips. I saw pitted ripples across my full thighs where they emerged through a slit in the side of the gown. I felt the softness of my belly beneath the braided gold belt and I felt the heaviness of my breasts rubbing against the soft fabric.

I was beautiful, too.

All around me was such stunning, hypnotic beauty that my eyes teared, and I blinked quickly to avoid ruining the kohl that the nymphs had drawn around my eyes.

"Oh, don't cry!" Thalia pleaded. "It really isn't that bad. He's not *cruel*, not like some of the others."

"Thalia!" Euphrosyne cried.

Thalia shrunk, but I spun to her. "What do you mean? Who isn't cruel?"

They shared another look. They had a language they communicated with brows and lips pursing and eyes widening.

After a moment, Euphrosyne sighed. "Ares, Goddess. He

desires you."

"And he's the god of war," Thalia said. "He always gets what he sets his sights on."

That feeling returned to my stomach. Unease. The way he had touched my arm, my breast, the texture of his gaze on me—it stoked that feeling higher.

My body did not know sex yet, but I knew of it the way I knew other things—the memories and ideas were within me, the world fully formed in my mind.

"Well, he will not have me," I told them. "I am a goddess, ranked alongside him."

Something else Thalia said caught me, and I gaped at her.

"How do you know he isn't cruel?"

She straightened my gown, flicked away a nonexistent speck, and smiled up at me. "We are nymphs," she said, as if that was explanation enough.

My heart bucked. "And what does that mean? You are disposable?"

I watched the idea play across her face, the contrasting fact that she was *not* disposable. "I—my lady," was all she managed, her eyes soft with confused wonder.

"How does it work, then? You belong to everyone in this mountain?" Heat pulsed in me, and it took me a moment to recognize it as anger.

Thalia's brows went up. "If we have pleased you, my lady, you are welcome to claim us as—"

"Then I claim you. As my attendants only. And you only need . . . *serve* . . . Ares again if you wish it."

Utter silence fell over the room. I looked at their faces; had I done wrong? Not even here for a day yet and I had already messed something up—

But then Euphrosyne beamed. "Well," she said to Thalia and Aglaea, "look at us! Attendants to the Goddess of Beauty and Love."

Aglaea giggled and clapped. Thalia turned her smile to me and mouthed *Thank you*.

I nodded, my uncertainty vanishing, and returned their smiles. "I have purpose here beyond warming beds, and so do you."

"Oh!" Thalia jumped back and smacked her hands together. "Of *course* you do! Oh, we're such fools—come, come!"

"But the wedding!" Euphrosyne cried. "We only have an hour—"

"And she is ready! This cannot wait. It's her *duty*, after all!"

"What duty?" My heart squeezed at that notion. A duty. A purpose.

Beauty. Love.

"This way!" Thalia beckoned, and I lifted the hem of my gown, Euphrosyne and Aglaea trailing behind.

Thalia led us through more winding halls, up wide and gorgeous staircases, past rooms laden with bodies strewn over chaises and blankets. Many we passed were dining and sipping from goblets, others lazily fucking, and my eyes widened at those. They did everything with the same unhurried air of boredom that I almost missed the fact that they were having sex at all.

"These are all gods, too?" I asked.

Aglaea nodded. "Some are nymphs, demigods. Most of who you see are like you, my lady."

The beauty if this place, the pristine perfection of it all, flooded me with the need to cry or dance or gush—but every god I saw looked utterly dulled. They were in this place of utmost glamor, and their eyes were half lidded. Some *yawned*.

Was this my destiny, too? To one day be unaffected by the scent of sugar and nectar on the air, the cast of light from magical beams, the shudder of the curtains and glint on the gold trimmings?

Thalia stopped before a closed door at the end of a long, long hall. This door was made of iron, thick and heavy, with a scene formed into it of endless bodies, one after another after another, each unique, men and women and children and more. Some wept, some prayed, some ate, some danced.

My hands came up to cover my lips. "What is this?"

Thalia had her hand on the doorknob. She pulled back at my question and her eyes hit the motif as if seeing it for the first time. "Oh. It's the orb room. This is all mortals, I guess?"

Aglaea shrugged. "I think so. It makes sense."

"How?" I asked.

"The orb in this room lets you—or other gods—see into Earth," Thalia explained. "You can use your gifts to affect mortal lives. Some gods take more *direct* involvement, but others prefer to only interact this way."

"If they interact at all," Euphrosyne said with a short giggle.

"Is it unusual to interact with mortals?" I eyed them.

Thalia bobbed her head noncommittally. "Yes and no. It depends. Ares *loves* getting involved—mortals are great at killing each other! Hades spends a lot of time grabbing up mortal souls. Demeter likes to see the crops she brings about. But others? They usually only go down to take mortals to their beds. It depends on how interesting Earth is being."

"But this is our purpose?" I couldn't stop staring at the motif on the door. Every time I tried to focus on Thalia or Aglaea or Euphrosyne, my eyes drifted back, hooked by the *detail* in each mortal body. One had a necklace of overlapping bands. A child grinned, toothy and large.

"I think so," Thalia said. She yanked hard to open the door. The fact that it stuck, that she had to put her whole weight into opening it, had my brow furrowing. It was not well-used, this room.

I was quickly coming to a realization about Olympus. About the surface-level frivolity here.

But I shoved it aside and brushed my fingers along the door as we entered. "Who made this? Do you know?"

Euphrosyne's nose scrunched. "Oh, that was Hephaestus. God of Blacksmithing or something. You won't have to worry about him—he never comes out of his forge."

"What? Why would I have had to worry about him?"

"He's a *god*. And, well—" Thalia ushered me into the room, but I lingered, running my hands over the work of art. That was what it was—this door was one of the most beautiful things I had seen yet, and I couldn't believe my nymphs weren't captivated by it too. "He's just . . . unnerving. He's so quiet."

"And *big*," Aglaea added.

"Ares is big," I said absently.

"Not like Hephaestus," said Euphrosyne. "Ares is tall. Hephaestus is . . . well, he swings a hammer all day! He's like a mountain. And he's always so dirty! All that soot."

"I don't think I've ever heard him speak," said Thalia. "It's not normal. He just . . . stands there, when Zeus makes him come out. He stands and watches then just *leaves*."

"It is weird." Aglaea shuddered. "Feels like he's planning something. I don't trust him."

I made a soft moan of acknowledgment, giving one last look to the door. I doubted their perception of Hephaestus was accurate—but I had little by which to go on when it came to other gods. Only Ares, with his possessive demeanor, and Hera, Artemis, the others who had watched my creation and let me walk the long way up, naked and exposed.

Finally, I entered, and saw what Thalia had mentioned.

It was a small room, by the standards of the others, round and dim save for a glowing orb that sat in the exact center on a pedestal. The light it emitted gave the whole area a soft blue aura, dreamlike, and I walked forward, one hand outstretched.

I knew what to do. As ingrained in me as my purpose, as the surety of beauty, I approached the orb, and laid my hand on it.

Immediately, the orb hummed and warmed beneath my palm, and a flurry of images hit me. People—mortals—in dozens of situations, farming and fighting and laughing and crying, in taverns and homes and fields and beaches. I knew them all unconsciously, names pulsing at each sight, but more filled my mind, more and more, a forceful wave that rose and rose and yanked me deeper—

I breathed, drawing that sweet nectar air deep into me, and the images slowed. One. Then another. Another.

Until a man's face pulled up. He was young—or I guessed he was, for a mortal—with cheeks still rounded, eyes still clear. He was at a banquet, fingering a plate of dates, his gaze pinned across the room.

The vision peeled back to show the object of his attention: a truly gorgeous young woman, with flaxen hair and sparkling eyes. Her body writhed in a dance, music lulling her movements, and the young man was completely transfixed on her. Not in the way Ares and the other gods had been on me; no, this was pure, adoration and appreciation and a little lust, yes, but mostly honor. He was amazed that he could watch someone so perfect, be near someone so ethereal.

His name came to me. *Paris.*

Her name. *Helen.*

I drew back, every nerve in my body feeling alive and thrumming, lit from within by a newly burning ember that this orb had placed inside of me.

This was my purpose. To watch over these mortals, to guide their lives to find beauty and love.

"Did you use your gift, my lady?" Euphrosyne asked.

The nymphs were behind me, gathered by the open door, and when I turned to face them, I thought I saw a flash in the hall, a shadow shifting.

I frowned at it, but there was no one.

"I haven't," I said. "I want to think on what best to do. I don't want to harm them."

There was a pause.

Then Thalia laughed, bright and true. "Oh, my lady! I will enjoy serving you. You are so *funny*."

Funny? But she said it in a way that seemed like a good thing, so when they dissolved in laughter, I managed a half smile.

As we left, I looked back at the orb once more.

Paris and Helen.

I would figure out the perfect way to bring beauty and love into their lives.

4

Hephaestus

In the time since I had crafted it, no one had ever looked at the door I had made.

It had to be a thing of honor, as everything in Olympus was. We had come to take art for granted, but I had still poured extra attention into the details of the mortals splayed on this iron, carefully illuminating each one based on people I saw when I touched the orb. Their expressions, their objects, their poses.

When I had installed it, even Zeus hadn't done more than give it a quick glance before he ducked into the room.

But her.

She lingered. Studied it. *Fawned* over it. And as I'd watched from the shadows farther up the hall, I'd been as consumed by the awe on her face as she was consumed by the thing I had made.

Now, I watched her get rushed back up the hall by the nymphs, their trilling voices trying too hard to sell her on the wedding. *Oh, it'll be so magical! They always are! Hurry, my lady—do you hear the music starting?*

I heard it. Felt the vibrations in the floor, where just below, the grand banquet hall would be bursting with honey-sweet flowers and vats of wine and gods already drunk and reveling. I couldn't remember who was getting married—I hadn't gotten an official invitation. But this was Olympus, and I was a god. I had as much right to be there as anyone.

But I could see the shocked, disgusted faces of my siblings and the other gods already. The shrill shrieks of the nymphs in their laps. The gentle, demeaning way Zeus would slap my shoulder and say *"How goes my bolts, Hephaestus? Better to use your time for those pursuits. This will only bother you. You remember how wild it gets."*

Tension wound in my gut. The heavy, irrepressible need to run back to my forge. I had been away too long, out *here*, in the gilded marble halls. The starkness of my greased skin, my stained leather apron, the drag of my iron boots on the floor was a jarring contrast to the ornate perfection here.

To the ornate perfection of *her*.

She would be at the wedding. A crown jewel who would draw more attention than the bride or any other guests. And I knew how the night would culminate. Did she? Had those twittering nymphs explained *anything* to her yet?

Did she care?

The only reason I believed that she was uncomfortable had been from the flash in her eyes when Ares had first approached her in the sea. Who was I to say that she didn't want the *activities* that the other gods reveled in?

I stepped out of the shadows and neared the door to the orb room, careful to keep the clanking of my iron boots as soft as possible. I had gotten good at walking stealthily in them, and rarely did anyone else come here, so I was in no danger of being seen.

I touched the spot on the door where her fingers had lingered. On the outline of a woman with a jar balanced on her head.

I knew as much about the new goddess as I knew about this woman—surface only. The level of superficiality that permeated the halls of Olympus, thick as smoke.

That was not acceptable.

I needed to know if that look on her face had been true, if she did not want the advances Ares had hinted at.

If she did want it, then I would slink back into the shadows.

But if she did not.

A bolt of possession grabbed my chest and tugged, hard, like two insistent hands.

No one else would intervene. No one else would stand up to my brother or any of the other gods. I had seen it—I *felt* it, the ache in my feet that would never go away, a permanent reminder of what happened when a god defied gods.

Even with that pain reminding me of what I could lose.

Even with my past mistakes ghosting after me.

I made my way down the hall, to the stairs, closer and closer to the celebration that shook the core of the mountain. Each step wrenched the breath in my lungs and cramped my stomach until I was all wound, a being of tension and strain.

This is a fool's errand. You would repeat history, and for what? Go back to your forge. Go back and accept that you can do nothing.

But I kept walking forward.

For her.

5

Aphrodite

The banquet hall was glorious.

There was no ceiling—an illusion, I knew, because we hadn't left the mountain; but there was a sky above us hung with white clouds, and all around the long, wide room were massive marble pillars of ivory striated with gold. Music played, a softly lulling tune, and tables sat everywhere, overflowing with the same delectable foods and drinks as had been scattered throughout the halls, to the point where I now began to wonder how this event was, actually, special. Through the beauty, I began to see the same opulent things I had seen already: fine silken drapes, gold trimmings, vases spewing lush fragrant flowers. And the beings already here—they were all dressed sumptuously, brilliant gowns and fine tunics and crowns of golden laurels.

They drank, and laughed, but the attitude was the same as I had seen in the rooms—tinged with boredom. Stifled yawns. They sipped and ate carelessly. A few lounged with others in their laps, but their attention never stayed on their partners for long.

I stood in the doorway, taking it all in, trying to reconcile the devastating beauty here with the just as overwhelming lack of appreciation. How could anyone be in this god-touched place and not *care*? Was there no one among the gods who would see or understand the beauty that pinned me in place? Even when I told my nymphs they could stay, they'd said that they'd been to weddings before, then patted my arms and retreated to my suite of rooms.

My mind flashed back to the door of the orb room. The care that had been taken to carve each mortal, to make them all unique.

Hephaestus.

I would have to meet him. I wanted to know if he had intentionally poured such beauty into that door, or if it had been a blithe effort from yet another god burdened with inconceivable boredom.

A coldness crept over me. That I would, one day, maybe, be just as empty as the beings around me. How long would my fascinations last?

The music stopped.

The abrupt pull of silence had me sipping in a quick breath, and in that flash, I felt the eyes of everyone in this room swivel to me.

Now, the energy changed.

Boredom raced away so efficiently I heard the scurry of its feet on the marble.

The eyes that watched took me in, head to toe, and even though I was dressed now, I felt naked all over again. I fought to keep from crossing my arms over my chest as I stepped farther into the room.

Rearing up again, I felt that primal drive from them that I

had felt before—*hunger*.

"Aphrodite!" Ares's voice boomed over the silence.

I couldn't suppress my shudder and twisted in his direction. The crowd parted, most faces bending quickly with jealousy; *ah, she has been claimed already.*

My lip flickered in a snarl. I would not play this game. I was not something to be fought over.

Ares stalked towards me, dressed in his own version of wedding garb. A gleaming golden breastplate over a pleated soldier's kilt with thick laced sandals that stretched up his lean calves. The sheen of his golden hair matched the luminescence on the breastplate, the same glint in his eyes, until if I let my gaze drift out, he was just a blur of gold, like a pulse of a sunbeam.

But he came upon me with such presence that I forced myself to stay focused on him. I was ready now for his behavior.

"Aphrodite," he said again and took my arm.

I deftly pulled out of his grip. "Ares."

Challenge flickered in his eyes. I thought I heard a gasp from the crowd.

Was it really that shocking that I might rebuff him?

I cast my gaze around the staring gods. "Where are those who would be married? I should greet them."

Ares's attention hung heavy on the side of my face. He was silent a beat too long. "Ah," he said. "Come. I will introduce you. There are many you should meet."

He extended his arm, an offering.

This time, I took it, because he hadn't forced me to it; but I still caught the smile of victory that flashed on his face as he paraded me through the room.

I heard their voices whisper my name. *That is Aphrodite. The*

Goddess of Beauty and Love.

Oh, she is lovely, isn't she?

How much does she know of love if she is so new, hm? A jibe said as someone elbowed their neighbor, as they cut a sly grin at me and thought I hadn't heard.

The apex of my thighs pulled. I had seen the thick curl of my hair, had quickly felt the soft, slick lips of my cunt while the nymphs dressed me. Yes, I was the goddess over sex, too; but I had not yet had sex, had I? I was goddess of something I did not know.

Ares made good on his promise and saw that I met everyone in the room. Names and faces began to blur, gods and goddesses and demigods and nymphs. The bride and groom, Peleus and Thetis, smiled beguilingly at me, but I could see the cut of anger in Thetis's eyes when she took in my figure, the way all in the room looked at me, not her.

"You are a vision," I told her, and meant it. She was as stunning as the room, draped in glistening aqua silk that accented a hue in her skin, made her shine rosy and plump.

Thetis's smile was flat. "Thank you." She turned to her betrothed. "Shall we have the ceremony?"

Peleus sipped wine and looked at the door. "Zeus is not—"

Trumpets sounded.

I twisted to look, Ares turning with me—he had not once let go of my arm—to see a great procession descending into the room through a massive archway. Servants and attendants aplenty rushed ahead, tossing flower petals to be crushed beneath the feet of who could only be Zeus. He was toweringly tall and muscularly thick, rivaling Ares in the breadth of his arms and thighs, with a long, heavy white beard strung with golden beads and gems. His blue eyes were whip-quick and alert, seeing us all in one sweep.

We were gods, but he was the god above all, and I felt the importance of his presence as I had felt every unspoken revelation this day.

Had it only been a day, truly? Time was strange here.

Zeus made straight for Ares.

For me, I realized.

He stopped before us. "Our newest addition. Welcome to Olympus, Aphrodite."

He had heard of me, then. Of course he had.

I bowed my head. "I am pleased to be here."

"Yes, yes." He turned, reaching for a goblet of blood red wine. When he faced me again, he sipped it, letting his eyes lazily travel the length of my body.

"Is Ares being a cordial guide?" Zeus asked, his gaze fixed on the low cut of my gown, the slice of bare skin between my breasts.

"When he cares to be," I admitted.

A pause.

Then a roar of laughter so strong Zeus sloshed wine down his beard. The stain didn't linger; an attendant dove forward and banished it with a wave of their hand.

"Stay on your guard, Ares!" Zeus said. "This one may yet flatten you."

Ares put his hand over my arm where it rested in the cradle of his. Did I imagine that the way he dug his fingers into my skin felt like a threat?

"I shall be most willing to let her drop me to my back," he said, and now not just Zeus laughed, but those in his group as well.

The god-king dropped his chalice of wine and an errant

servant scrambled to catch it. "Now, what is the cause of today?"

A bolt of horror struck through me.

Zeus had come here—and greeted me first. Not the bride or groom.

I threw a look over my shoulder, at Peleus and Thetis, to see Thetis scowling at me with such fiery hatred that I felt the hair at the edges of my scalp begin to burn. I tried to show her my apology in the wideness of my face, but she only glared deeper, fuming, until Zeus turned to her.

"Ah, yes. You wish to be married, hm?"

Peleus stepped forward. "Yes, my lord."

"Well then. Let us get on with it."

It was a simple affair. We did not sit to witness it; barely the party of the room stilled. Peleus and Thetis faced each other and Zeus proclaimed them wed beneath him and that was that.

I was winded by the time Peleus and Thetis, arm in arm, began to walk the room, thanking their guests for coming.

"That is all?" I asked Ares.

He still had not left my side. "For the ceremony. The true event comes in moments."

"True event?"

"Let it begin!" Zeus boomed from across the room. He sat on a wide, curling chaise, lounged with one leg lifted.

I eyed Ares.

His grin was ferocious to the point I felt my stomach sink, like I had been made a fool of somehow.

The musicians—I could not see where they were, but the music emanated to every corner—played a new song, something low and sultry and lovely. It made my breath catch, the beauty of it distracting me enough that I allowed Ares to pull me to the corner where Zeus was, where all the guests now funneled into an arrangement of chaises and cushioned chairs that attendants scrambled to position.

All of it faced a center circle.

Ares pulled the two of us to the front row. A quick glare at a lesser goddess had her fleeing a narrow chaise, and he sat first.

Then pulled me into his lap.

I started to rise, but he clung tight to my hips, his strong fingers pressing in, pulling.

"Ah-ah," he growled into my neck. "This is the best seat in the room, Beauty. Stay and watch."

"Do not call me—"

A flash of light silenced me.

In the center circle, where previously there had been nothing, appeared a bed. Elevated so all could see, the bed was covered in soft white sheets.

Thetis and Peleus approached it. She shot me yet another tight glare, unhappy to see me so close. And I was close—close enough that I could see the tent of Peleus's erection, could feel the gust of Thetis's exhale when he deftly undid the knot at the back of her gown and the top fell down.

The crowd of gods stilled. Only the music gave sound to this, my breath tangled in my chest alongside my traitorous heart that could not decide whether to race or thud heavily.

Thetis's beauty only grew as Peleus undressed her at the foot of the bed. She stepped to remove her gown, balanced to disrobe, willingly submitting to this, until she was naked before us all, before every god in Olympus.

"What are they doing?" I hissed the question, half to myself, half to Ares.

"Consummating their marriage," Ares whispered, his lips

against the shell of my ear.

I could feel his own growing erection against the swell of my ass. I went as still as possible, not wanting any movement to give him incentive.

Peleus grabbed Thetis's shoulders and twisted her to face him.

Across from me, directly, was Zeus, his eyes hooded as he watched the groom fondle his new wife's breasts. They were small, perky, with large pink nipples that Peleus circled with his index finger. He pinched one, then the other, making them stand hard and straight, only to trace circles around them again, softening them. He teased her like this for minutes that stretched on until I realized I hadn't breathed with watching the torment.

I knew, somehow, the idea of being touched like that, and I could feel the visceral reaction in my own body as I watched Thetis whimper and writhe and fight to hold still. All I wanted suddenly was to touch myself as she was being touched. Would it truly feel that good? Was this body I had so recently been created into capable of the same sensations? What else could it do?

My cunt was growing wet. The dampness of it reminded me—I was on Ares's lap. Would he feel it? Would he take it as invitation? But I was spellbound by the flush creeping across Thetis's chest, the way I could see every shuddering effect of her breath as her body trembled beneath her husband's ministrations. Her jaw was clenched tight, but that too eventually softened, lips parting until she made a throaty, choked moan.

"Is she wet?" someone called from the back, and a riot of cheers and whistles lit the air.

That question broke the intensity that hung over the room, the same intensity that had left me breathless. What had been briefly reverent immediately took a twist of that prowling hunger I was coming to hate.

"Fuck her!" someone else called.

Peleus's eyes cut to Zeus.

He needed approval?

Zeus watched Thetis, watched her the way Ares had watched me.

"Beg me," he said. To her.

Peleus took his wife's chin in his thumb and finger and turned her face to him. I could not see what expression she wore from this angle, but I saw the relaxed set of her shoulders, her hands, the way she still shuddered breath.

And I heard the desperation in her voice when she said, "Please, Zeus. Let him fuck me."

Another series of whistles. Another outburst of cheers. Ares was one of them.

Zeus nodded, his eyes darkening.

Peleus pushed Thetis flat on the bed. Her legs spread immediately, and from where Ares had chosen to sit, we did have the best view. Her cunt glistened, open before us, that small, gaping hole parting wide as she hooked her hands beneath her knees and stretched herself, showing a drop of white moisture dripping down to her asshole.

"Fuck me," she begged. "Peleus—*please*."

The cheers and whistles rose again.

"Show us the cock, Peleus!"

"What's she begging for, eh?"

Peleus disrobed, and while I had no experience with cocks yet, I knew looking at him that it was mediocre. If Thetis was disappointed, she didn't show it; she kept her legs spread, her body flushed, her nipples pebbled and red.

Peleus lined his cock with her entrance and thrust inside without pretense. She cried out, head lolling back, and as he began to fuck her in earnest, her cries were a little forced, a little performative, until it rocked something loose in my brain.

She had faked all of this. She wasn't upset by it, but she wasn't enjoying herself to the degree she had let us believe.

The crowd was, though.

A few already had their cocks or cunts out, nymphs or servants open-mouthed between their knees, and I had a spark of panic that these nymphs were like *my* nymphs, and had not been given a choice.

But as I turned, scanning the crowd, Ares ran his hand up my back and yanked the top of my gown down my arms, exposing my breasts to the room.

Panic chilled me.

"Ares!" I scrambled for the straps of fabric, but he kept them pinned, using them as braces to hold my arms down. The fabric bit into my forearms and he twisted his grip, tightening it even more.

The bride and groom still fucked, Peleus continuing to drive into Thetis, wet slaps as she faked moans and pinched her own nipples.

But the eyes of the crowd spun from the fucking couple to me.

Whispers rippled around us. The whistles directed at Peleus and Thetis pivoted, and the catcalls followed suit. Zeus flicked his eyes to me, and a smile of interest dragged across his face.

A headiness twisted, and I had the sudden, lightning-bright fear that everyone in this room was imagining me in that position, spread on a bed, getting fucked and moaning.

I barely knew what my own body was capable of—and all these beings had laid claim to me somehow, to that reaction, before I even truly knew it.

Ares grabbed one breast, pinched my nipple, and I shrieked, fighting to stand.

"Don't play coy, Goddess," he hissed, holding me fast. "I have seen everything you have already. And you are the Goddess of Love, are you not? Show me what love is, Beauty."

One hand still holding the straps of fabric as restraints, he dove his other hand beneath the waist of my gown, my gold belt a sad shield, and expertly plunged two fingers into my wet, virgin cunt.

I seized his wrist with a startled cry at the invasion. My mouth went dry, my body too delicate, my heart beating too fast—

No, I wanted to say, I tried to say, but I was pinned and breathless with the feel of his fingers inside of me, with how raw and sensitive that part of my body could be.

I had wanted to find out what else my body could do.

But not like this.

A god next to him leaned over. "Look at these breasts, Ares!"

He reached for me, for my breast, and Ares leaned back, using his fingers in my cunt and the straps of my gown to steer my body towards the interloper.

The god palmed my breast, tweaked my nipple, and I choked, stunned, gone to full immobility at the horror of how quickly this had happened. Ares slid his fingers out, back in, pumping forcefully as the other god rolled the bud of my nipple between his thumb and finger. My body betrayed me and I felt a gush of warmth against Ares's fingers.

I was a goddess, wasn't I?

And yet I was powerless, utterly, even in my own body's reactions.

"Goddess of Beauty indeed," the god muttered. "How she's feel, Ares? Dripping?"

Ares twisted me away from the other god and ripped his hand out of my cunt. He held up his glistening fingers. "I'd say so," he declared, showing the juices to the gods next to him, to Zeus, who chuckled and rubbed at the bulge of his tunic.

I flew to my feet, feeling outside of myself, a soul hovering. Ares let me take a step away, too intent on the wetness of my cunt on his fingers.

Most seemed to have forgotten about Peleus and Thetis. Her eyes met mine as her husband continued to idly fuck her, and still she glared at me, that jealous hatred sharp and vile.

Everywhere I looked, I saw only jealousy or hunger.

I spun, tugging the straps of my gown up, shaking hands losing grip only to fumble and right the fabric, but I was disheveled. What if I called for my nymphs? Would they be able to help? Would anyone?

This was the reality I had been created into.

This was the world I occupied now.

A goddess of beauty was as good as a lamb in this den of wolves.

Ares stood. "Let me welcome you to Olympus properly. Others deserve a chance, too—we share and share alike here, and you, darling, will not be selfish, will you?"

"Strip her!" the god who had grabbed my breast called.

Ares reached for me again. Snatched the fabric of my gown. I ducked beneath his arm and *ran*.

Something ripped—the back of my gown, until I felt the

fabric go limp; I held it to me and kept my head low and sprinted through the rows of gods and goddesses and fucking. It had devolved into an orgy, and even though most had been watching Ares expose me, everyone was preoccupied with their own pleasure, and so only a few hands groped for me as I bolted, but none found purchase.

I stumbled free of the crowd and sprinted across the open marble towards the archway on the far wall.

"Whoever catches her, claims her!" Zeus bellowed.

Feet stomped, chairs peeled as they were shoved across the floor.

I ran, tears building, terror piercing straight to my core. Where would I go? Where was safe? I barely knew this place—could I even find my way back to my room?

I bolted into the hall, breathless, holding the scraps of my gown to my breasts—

And immediately bounced off a wall.

This—this had been a hall, hadn't it?

I faltered back, briefly disoriented.

And looked up.

And up.

And up.

Into a chiseled, dark face lined with a short brown beard, black eyes fixed on me. Thick, cut muscles flooded with bulging veins ran down massive his shoulders and arms and legs beneath a leather apron and a short pleated kilt. He had a hammer in one clenched hand and a ferocity in his dark eyes that I hadn't seen yet—not hunger, not desire, not possession.

Rage.

Manic, peppered *fury*.

I glanced back at the archway. Feet thundered closer.

I had seconds, maybe.

"Please," I begged. I had nothing else to give. I doubted I could escape this god, not with his size and the sheer breadth of him; I couldn't cut around him, couldn't go back the way I'd come without crossing in front of the banquet room. But he hadn't been in the orgy, so maybe, maybe— "Please help me. *Please.*"

6

Hephaestus

res was lucky he was buffeted by the whole of the crowd.

He was lucky I had not seen what was happening until she stood, and turned, and the look on her face unraveled every remaining instinct of restraint I had left.

I was nearly into the room, hammer ready, when she fled. And now, staring down at her small body, the frantic way she tried to hold her ruined gown over her nakedness, the *terror* in her eyes, I became the very thing my siblings always mocked me for being: a monster.

"Get behind me," I told her, a vicious growl.

She hesitated only a moment.

Then she nodded and obeyed, rushing around and pressing herself to my back.

I could feel her shaking.

Hear her too-quick gulps of breath.

I wanted to turn, to take her into my arms and hold her fast until her trembling stopped.

But we were no longer alone.

Ares was first out of the room. On his heels came others—Apollo, Dionysus, more far beneath us who sought to scoop up whatever scraps my brothers would leave for them.

And scraps they would leave.

Ares pulled up short at the sight of me. "Ah, Hephaestus. Crawled out of your hole, did you?"

My knuckles compressed around the hammer. "The chase is over."

"Excuse me?" Ares cocked his head. "What do you even know about—"

"I said," I cut him off, voice a roar, "the chase is over."

And I turned, sweeping my arm around her shoulders.

The moment they saw her, where she had been cowering behind me, a gasp rippled through them.

Then a growl.

I felt Ares's hand on my arm, bearing down.

I whirled, hefting my hammer through the air, using the momentum gained in the spin to heave it straight at his head.

He ducked just in time, one arm coming up to fend off the back blow.

We'd sparred too much when we were younger. He knew my tells; I knew his.

So we froze, him up and ready, me holding my hammer out.

Behind me, in the cradle of my other arm—she hadn't moved away, and trembled still—she watched us, and I felt the puff of her startled exhale.

"The fuck are you doing, Hephaestus?" Ares snarled.

"You heard our almighty," I said. "Whoever catches her, claims her. She's mine."

The color drained from Ares's face only to rise again almost instantly, a flare of furious red. "You *fucker*," he snarled.

But a bark of laughter shattered whatever he had planned to do next.

"Well, *this* is a change!" Zeus's voice carried. The cluster of gods parted for him, their eyes seething on me, but Zeus's face was all amusement. "Clever Hephaestus. You won her, fair and outright."

"You cannot condone this!" Ares shouted.

Zeus's amusement hardened.

When he turned to Ares, my brother realized his slip up and ducked his head, lip curling even so.

"He won," Zeus declared. "When he tires of her, you may try again, Ares. He deserves to have his fun as much as any of us, eh?"

Zeus nodded at me. He didn't even look down at her. Didn't once ask if she wanted this fate, if she was *all right*.

She was clearly not all right.

I lowered my hammer, pressed it to my side, muscles coiled in barest control.

"Enjoy, Hephaestus," Zeus said placidly.

He turned, and swept back into the banquet room. Within, a cry went up, the pinging squeal of someone in orgasm—the orgy had continued, no cares given.

Slowly, the group followed Zeus back in.

Until only Ares remained.

He dropped his glare from me to her and I stepped into his vision, creating a shield of my body.

He spoke to her anyway. "You could have had me, Beauty. This deformed beast is what you get for running."

I felt her jolt at the sound of his voice. Or was it what he said?

Either way, I snarled at him. "Leave. Now."

Ares eyed me once more. With a scoff, he trudged back into the banquet hall.

She released a quick breath in his absence. "Thank you," she whispered.

But still, she trembled.

She was afraid of me.

"Come," I told her and started off. I kept my arm around her, my skin hovering just above hers, not trusting that Ares or some other wayward god would not dart out and snatch her away.

She followed, arms curled around herself, her eyes fixed to the floor as we walked. Occasionally, she would steal a look up at me, her body shaking and twitching so she made contact even when I tried to keep from touching her.

Just that barest touch. Just the roughness of my calloused fingers on her silken skin.

I was in a fog. Delirium thickening.

The smallest spark of victory burned in my chest: I had protected her. They had not ruined her.

I wasn't sure what to do with this feeling, something like vindication—but on its heels came a surge of realization that this victory was not forever. Ares would be waiting, stalking, driven to the hunt even more now.

How would I keep her safe once she was away from me? What more could I do to ensure that she stayed out of their clutches?

A plan formed. Slowly. Daringly. This small win had awakened some of my former boldness, and I anchored to it.

We walked silently through the meandering halls, down staircases, until we reached the door of the suite she had been given.

I opened it for her.

She blinked, startled, and for the first time since running into me, she looked up with clear eyes.

"You brought me to my rooms," she stated.

I nodded.

"Thank you," she said, with more conviction.

I grunted, the doorknob warming under my hand.

She paused on the threshold. Beyond, I could hear her nymphs giggling in one of her branching rooms.

"What does this mean," she started, her voice breathy, "that you have claimed me?"

"It means they did not."

She tipped her head. Waiting. "That's all?"

"I am not going to force myself on you, if that is what you mean."

Her eyebrows lifted. She studied my face, and I held under her scrutiny, growing more shocked each passing second that she didn't flinch or recoil.

I had a permanent burn on my cheeks from the forge. My skin was not sun-kissed like the others, but nut brown from my work. Grease and dirt streaked on my body from an unfinished project on my anvil. And her eyes dropped lower, taking in all of me, until she caught on my iron boots, on the braces that I had fashioned, the only things that let me walk.

Her eyes returned to mine, her face gentle. "Zeus called you Hephaestus."

"Hm."

"You made the door? To the orb room."

A hot breath pulsed out of my nose. "Yes."

She smiled.

It was the sun.

It was the rush of rightness when I knew I had completed a project, the stunning satisfaction in absolute perfection.

I was rendered dumb beneath it, lips parting, a weak, guttural moan palpitating in my throat.

"It's amazing," she said, her voice a brush of noise. "The details. The skill. How did you make each person look so unique?"

"I used their references from the orb. They are all living mortals. Or were—their lives do not last long."

"You use the orb?"

I nodded. "Few believe that mortals are capable of true creation, of high skill—but many have shown to be exceptional. I guide their progresses as I am able."

She studied me, something unreadable in her eyes. I realized she was waiting for a catch, for me to scoff or laugh it off.

But when I held, her smile widened.

I would live the rest of my endless days and never again see something so enrapturing.

"The door you made is a beautiful tribute to them," she said.

"From you," I whispered, "that is the highest praise."

"You know who I am?"

I nodded again.

She cupped the straps of her gown in one hand to press her other palm against her chest. "Aphrodite," she said anyway, an introduction.

One half of my lips tilted up. It had been so long, ages upon ages, since I had smiled, that I didn't recognize the act at first.

I put a hand on my chest. "Hephaestus. But you know that."

"It's lovely to meet you," she said. "And I actually mean it."

That hand on my chest clenched into a fist. I lowered it to

my side.

"Thank you again," she said and started into her room.

But she held, her back to me, the sharp angles of her bare shoulders stiff, the swoop of her lower back sheened with sweat.

I had the sudden urge to drop to my knees and feather kisses down that curve, worship her flawlessness, but it was fantasy, that she would ever allow me that luxury. Already I had pushed my luck when I had cupped my arm around her.

Her chin tipped, showing her in profile. "It is difficult," she started, "to figure out what mark I am meant to make on our world when I am constantly dodging attacks."

"You have had a poor introduction to your eternity."

She laughed.

The sound went straight to my half-hard cock, and I was so grateful she was faced away from me and couldn't see the bulge growing against my apron.

"How long will your claim on me last?" she asked.

"How long do you want it to?"

It was an impossible question. An even more impossible answer. She would recoil now, realize what she was giving up—Ares had attempted to force himself on her, but there were plenty still she could take as more viable lovers, less grotesque partners.

Her chin lifted. Her lips parted. "Long enough," was all she said, but she said it like a prayer, with the same wistfulness that echoed in my chest.

Then she was gone, slipping into her room, and I shut the door behind her.

I leaned my forehead against it. Breathed in deep through my nose, out through my mouth.

The plan that had begun to take root started to blossom.

I knew of only one way to ensure that this feeble claim I had would protect her fully. One act that would seal her as *mine*, regardless of any physical tie between us.

Based on the way Zeus and Ares and the rest had treated her like an object with no regard to her feelings, I suspected I could play their game against them and enact this without her even knowing, extend this net of safety around her from afar so she could find her footing on Olympus without threat of assault or manipulation. Then, when she had figured out her role among us, I could dissolve it, with her never having to know it had been there at all.

Heart in my throat, a lump I couldn't dislodge, I turned from her room and made for Zeus.

7

Aphrodite

My nymphs were shocked to see me back.

"It can't be over already!" Euphrosyne cried.

Thalia scrambled up from where they lounged before an open set of balcony doors. Beyond, I saw the sea, heard the crash and burble of waves, and I stood staring out at the sky for a moment, breathing, breathing.

"Here, my lady." Thalia handed me a new gown. Her gentle fingers pulled at the scraps I held to my chest, and I let her undress me, then slipped into the new garment, something simple, a belted gown of pleated orange.

"How was it?" Aglaea leaned over, chin propped on her hands. "How was *he?*"

"Aglaea!" Euphrosyne giggled and smacked her. "Have decency!"

I barely heard them, in truth.

I saw only Thalia, who studied me, and her face bowed slightly.

"She does not have to tell us," she snapped at them. "Up, both of you—we will prepare her bed. She has had a long day."

The three of them filed out into another room—I hadn't even seen every room in this suite I had been given—but I stood still, watching the sky, listening to the sea.

No one here cared for the tasks we had been given. Purposes were as frivolous as everything else. Nothing had *meaning*, nothing demanded *respect*, no one *cared—*

Though that wasn't true. Was it?

He cared.

He was so different from everything else in Olympus, in every possible way. Dirty where everything was clean; dark where everything was forced into light; and kind. Kind, where nothing, *nothing*, had shown even a flicker of consideration.

And he was relegated to a forge, the nymphs had said. Outcast among the gods.

What was his eternity like? Hiding away, creating unappreciated works of art, the passage of time drawing him closer and closer to . . . nothing.

I could not live like this. I could not *exist* like this, for what we had was not even living. It was pointless and stupid if the other gods truly thought that boredom was the utmost we could strive for.

But I would not accept banishment, either.

Hephaestus's claim on me had stopped the chase. Had stopped Ares. And the way he had led me here, escorted me safely back to my rooms, and seemed actually aghast at having to tell me that he was *not* going to assault me . . . even if nothing else about him had been attractive, that would have been enough.

As it was, I had not breathed properly since seeing him in that hall. Each shuddering twitch that had bumped me into his extended arm had speared lightning to my core, and if I had been less shaken by what had happened in the banquet room, I would have pressed myself into him for a different reason.

Whoever catches her, claims her. She's mine.

What does this mean, that you have claimed me?

It means they did not.

I crossed back into the room where the nymphs had readied me. A table sat beside the tall mirror, laden still with makeup.

I grabbed the jar of kohl and dug my fingers into the black paste, smearing it over my hand.

Hephaestus's claim on me would hold—for how long? He had offered it. I did not know the rules, not entirely. But I did not want to be dependent on his mere presence to walk through what was supposed to be my home now.

And, deeper, I had wanted his hands on me.

The thought reawakened that moment when Thetis had been naked before Peleus, and his fingers had played with her breasts, and I had lost myself in the allure of it, in the potential of what it might feel like to touch and be touched like that. But what I still had was the lingering remnants of Ares's force on me, the memory of his fingers in my cunt—the first that had ever been there.

I needed to reclaim myself.

I needed to make this body mine, not theirs.

And what I wanted it to be was touched by . . . *him.*

There had been grease stains on his fingers. Embedded under his nails.

And so as I dragged my kohl-smeared hand across my upper arm, I briefly let myself imagine it was him. His touch. The grind of his thick fingers bearing down on my soft skin.

I drew away and eyed the marks in the mirror. They looked like fingerprints—too thin to really be his, but enough, I hoped, to make Ares or any other god think twice before touching what did not belong to them.

The thought did not appall me like it had with Ares. The idea of being claimed by Hephaestus left me . . . breathless.

I watched my kohl-black fingers in the mirror.

Watched as I untied the belt with my clean hand and peeled down the straps of my gown and let the fabric fall until I was naked again, this time in the first moment of privacy I had been given.

I trailed my fingers over one nipple, mimicking the way Peleus had touched Thetis. Pinching, circling, pinching again, and my breath sharpened, nipples hardening in my own excitement so I could not get them to soften.

The kohl smeared around and around.

I moved to my other breast, the one that had been groped by the god I did not even know, and I did what he had done, reclaiming the sensation by rolling that pebbled bud between my fingers.

Tension wound in my chest, shot down into the pit of my belly. He had been too rough—a gentle squeeze at the very tip was all that was needed, the slightest twist of my fingers, and I was reeling, drowning in an effervescence that had me moaning faintly into my clamped lips.

I reached for the jar of kohl again and reapplied more to my hand. Both breasts were decorated in smears of black now, looking like that great blacksmith god had taken his liberties after all.

I bit down another moan, a brittle, wicked whimper, and spread my thighs to see that dampness still, glistening like the sea.

I pressed my hand to my cunt's lips, holding there, feeling

where Ares's fingers had been. I delved in, touching away the remnants of him, and pushed two fingers inside, then three, and pumped, pumped again, biting my lip at the rising of sensation. My body was warm still from everything that had happened, excitement peaking immediately, brought back to the surface when I saw the smears of kohl against my delicate skin and I imagined, *I imagined*, this hand was Hephaestus, what his brutal fingers might feel like inside of me.

Warmth grew, and grew, and I kept my eyes on myself in the mirror. My cheeks flushed so red they purpled, mouth in a desperate, seeking *O*, eyes pinching in something that bordered on pain, but it was need only, raw and hungering.

I slid my wet fingers out and touched the spot at the apex of my cunt, the button to which all these sensations funneled. When I pressed it, a current roared through my limbs, every nerve springing in quaking throbs that I chased by rubbing the nub in tight, hard circles, until that building storm crashed upon me in wave after wave of roiling euphoria.

The aftermath had me gasping, limbs quaking in liquid satisfaction.

I had wondered what else my body was capable of.

This—this was beauty, love incarnate, a riot of all I was goddess over. That such ecstasy could be reached—were all gods capable of this? But I knew they were, our bodies were not that different. They could do this, and yet they wasted their time in boredom? How could anyone grow bored of *this*?

I hated them all.

Almost.

As I withdrew my hand, I stared at the smears of black all around my cunt, the fingerprints on my nipples, the streak on my arm like I had been grabbed.

How much better would orgasm feel when given by someone else?

These pretend marks of Hephaestus on my nipples and cunt would be just for me. Unless Ares took it too far—and then I could throw my head back and claim that the god he had scowled at was the most superior lover, that Hephaestus had marked himself upon me, and I had let him.

I cleaned my hands on a towel, forcing steadying breaths, and drew my gown back up, belted it around my waist.

I was shaking a little now, the aftershocks making my body overly sensitive, but each one had me whimpering with wanting *more*. With wanting to have that plunging fullness thrusting within me while I came hard and bright—

Later. In the privacy of my bedchamber, perhaps.

Or I could find this forge.

Thank him again.

I shivered, eyes sliding shut, and drew in another fortifying breath.

There was something I needed to do first.

"Thalia," I called.

Moments later, she popped her head into the room.

"I would like to go to the orb room," I told her.

She gave a startled blink. "Of course. One moment."

She set down a stack of sheets she had been holding and told the other two nymphs to keep readying the bedchamber.

Her eyes dropped to the smear on my arm as she ushered me out the door. "My lady?"

"Hephaestus claimed me," I told her.

"Not Ares?"

I nodded.

Thalia's eyes went wide, a flash of surprise laced with fear.

But she turned, and we walked in silence for a minute.

Then I felt her gaze on the side of my face. "Are you all right, my lady?"

I let her see my clear eyes, my calm smile. "I am. He did not harm me."

Her brow creased. "He . . . didn't? Did you want him to claim you, my lady?"

"No."

She blinked quickly, like she could not piece together the right question, nor any sort of answer.

"I don't understand, Goddess," she said finally. "But if you are all right . . . if Hephaestus comes to your room. Should we permit him to enter?"

"Yes," I said, and my throat tightened.

Would he?

I doubted it. He did not seem the sort to be as bold as Ares, as commanding.

"And yet you didn't want him to claim you. But he didn't harm you." Thalia shook her head. "You have made Olympus very interesting already, my lady."

I cut a smile as we continued down the halls.

At the orb room, I slipped within, Thalia lingering for me outside.

The room was empty. I doubted I would ever find it occupied—no matter. I would do my duty, fulfill my purpose, the other gods be damned.

I approached the orb and laid my palm on it. Instantly, I was swarmed with the sights and emotions of thousands of mortals, but I clamped my eyes shut and called for the two I had seen.

Paris. Helen.

They were in bed together. His arm was around her waist, their eyes shut in blissful sleep, naked limbs twisted in strewn sheets.

They had found their way to each other, then, without my involvement. But I wanted to be sure their love lasted, even if things in their world set against them.

My eternity was in question, safety not guaranteed; but for them, for these fragile mortals, I could give that certainty.

So I pushed the breadth of my power towards them: that the beauty of their love would endure above all.

That was the gift I gave them. The blessing of a goddess.

8

Hephaestus

The orgy raged still.

Part of me whispered that I needed to accept this feeble victory and retreat. She was safe—for now—what more could I really do? I was pressing my luck, and hers.

But the rest of me crossed the banquet room, sidestepping fucking groups.

At the edge of my vision, I spotted Ares, balls-deep in a demigod with huge breasts.

My gaze sought out Zeus, and I fixed to him.

I would not lose. Not again.

Not this time.

Not her.

I stopped beside the chaise on which our god-king sprawled. He was naked, and for once, the woman fucking him was his wife. Hera, too, was nude, her breasts bouncing as she thrust up and down on his cock.

But she was looking at a nearby couple, a nymph teasing the cunt of another in ravenous licks; and Zeus had his hand around the stiff cock of Peleus. Zeus and Hera seemed only vaguely aware of the fact that they were fucking each other at all.

Zeus's eyes trailed to me.

His brows twitched. He looked behind me, back to my face. "Did she remind you how much fun Olympus can be? I'll have to thank her. Collect her and join us."

"No," I managed.

He continued to stroke Peleus, but his attention was on me, even as his own cock was being milked by his wife's pussy.

How everyone else could still give themselves over to group sex was beyond me—there was nothing sensual to it, nothing revered. It was act and act alone.

"I have a request," I said. *A demand*, but I kept my face level.

"Oh?" His breath hitched as Hera bent forward, getting a better view of the nymphs.

"I would like you to marry me to Aphrodite."

I said it low enough—or thought I did—but I felt the pull of attention.

Others realized I was here. My presence alone was startling enough; but what I said hung in the air.

Ares was farther across the room. He wouldn't have heard. Still, I fought not to look at him.

Zeus shoved Peleus away and sat up, pushing his hands against Hera's hips.

"Go—you, *go*," he said absently, and she rolled her eyes and stood. His cock bobbed free, but his focus on me was all confusion, trying to read the truth on my face.

He would read nothing.

Finally, he laughed. "Well, Hephaestus. This is certainly . . . a surprise."

"How? I claimed her. She is mine. I am furthering my claim—marry us."

"What? Now?"

"Yes."

"She is not present."

"Need she be? You have married others like this before. Declare us married and be done with it."

Zeus scratched his chin, the grit of his beard sounding like the crinkle of paper. His eyes narrowed. "You have never shown interest in anyone before. Well—that is not true, is it? How long has it been?"

Do not speak of it. *Do not speak of it.*

He shrugged. "You propose an event, Hephaestus. You must see that. That *you*, our recluse, would marry!"

He said it loud.

Loud enough that the room would have heard.

Out of the corner of my eye, I saw Ares's head twist towards us.

I stiffened, hands balling tight. Luckily I had sheathed my hammer. "Will you consent to it?"

Zeus stood. The look on his face took on something grim, something dark. "I will."

I kept my exhale of relief capped. I did not like the gleam in his eye.

"But we will do this right," he told me. "It will be a celebration."

"No—" I said, too quickly, not catching myself in time.

Zeus frowned. "Is there a reason you would not want to celebrate your love? With the Goddess of Love, no less! No, Hephaestus—this is a cause for true joy. We will celebrate with you. A wedding."

But the darkness that lingered in his smile told me what he truly wanted: to see the consummation. To watch her get fucked.

I swallowed, my throat swelling. "I have never asked anything of you. I am owed one favor at least."

"Are you?" Zeus stepped closer. He was taller than me, only just, but I was thicker, and so I stood my ground. "I do not believe so, Hephaestus. This is my ruling. You will wed her tomorrow, and we will all be there to celebrate."

This plan had hinged on Zeus not caring for Aphrodite's opinion.

I had not taken into account the depth of his desire to see her exposed.

Stupid, *stupid* to underestimate him—

But I felt a presence at my side. "Who will the Soot God wed?"

Zeus smiled charmingly at Ares. "Aphrodite, of course."

I did not look to see his reaction.

I felt it.

The air hardened like the pause before a clap of thunder.

"And you tolerate this, Zeus?" Ares's words were carefully capped.

Zeus's grin was wide and manic. He knew exactly what he was doing to Ares. "I do. Does it bother you that much? You will still see her spread and mounted. Perhaps Hephaestus will even share her." He winked at me.

But there was weight to it.

Demand.

You will *share her.*

My jaw tensed. "What is mine remains mine alone. No one else will touch her."

Zeus's teasing manipulation flickered. He waited for me to relent, to bow to him like we always did.

But I held his gaze. Fury centered me.

"We will wed," I stated. "You will get your ceremony. But she is *mine*. You declared it."

I stormed off, rage heating up my neck, over my head, down my face until I saw everything through a sheen of red.

She wasn't supposed to know.

She was supposed to be blanketed by what protection I could offer from afar.

But now.

Now, we would be wed, in a ceremony and celebration as farcical as this one, and at the end of it—

How could I get her out of it?

Could I refuse the consummation? If I did, the bigger question: could I get her out of the banquet room and to safety before the crowd riled themselves to anger at being denied the consummation? What security waited for her if we ran—would my claim on her, our marriage, be treated as valid? Would I be able to protect her, or would all of this be for nothing if we didn't go through with it?

I stumbled into the hall and ground my fist into the wall, steadying myself. My feet ached and I willed myself to take another step, but I couldn't, I couldn't face what I had done.

All I had wanted was to protect her.

And now, I would be the monster she most feared, the one who had forced himself on her in every way.

9

Aphrodite

Gods and goddesses did not *need* sleep, but we still benefited from rest, or so the nymphs said. At their prodding—mostly Thalia's, who seemed to sense my mood best of all—I spread out on the massive bed they had prepared, intending to merely lie down for a bit.

But after the taxing weight of this day, my first and only so far, I should not have been surprised when darkness peeled back from me sometime later. I felt myself rise up out of unconsciousness the same way I had stepped from creation—a push and surge of life, ripples of color battering my eyelids, and then the smell of something rich that made my mouth water, the silken glide of the sheets on my naked form.

I pulled on a robe and rose, and found my nymphs in the front room, seated around a table set with all manner of pastries and steaming porcelain cups.

"My lady!" Aglaea cried. "We feared we allowed you to push yourself too hard yesterday—you have been asleep for nearly as long as mortals!"

"What is it they need?" Euphrosyne squinted. *"Fourteen*

hours of sleep? Or is it days?"

Thalia gave her an exasperated smile. "Hardly, but—my lady, come! We have food waiting, and drink."

I sat and took the small plate Aglaea made for me. Flaky tarts piled with fruit under a sheen of sugary glaze—I took a bite, and *oh*. The single orgasm I had had was divine, but this was an orgasm in and of itself, some rush of euphoria that had my eyes rolling back.

"So good, isn't it?" Aglaea grinned. "Demeter grows all the food herself—it's unmatched!"

"How would you know?" Thalia chastised. "Eaten much on Earth, have you?"

"I *imagine* it's better—it must be! We don't—"

"Oh!" Thalia jolted upright, splashing coffee from her small cup. "Oh, my lady! You had a visitor while you slept!"

I finished the last bite of the tart and lifted my brows at her. My stomach sank. "Ares?"

"Oh, heavens, no—well, yes, actually, but we did not believe you would care to know that he came? Anyway, it wasn't him I thought you would like to know about—it was Hephaestus."

That had my body going remarkably still. "Hephaestus?"

"Yes, Goddess." Aglaea grinned. "He looked quite . . . upset, actually. Fawning over you, I imagine!"

"We hardly know that," Thalia tried, gauging my reaction.

But I set down my plate and echoed Aglaea's grin. "Upset, hm?"

"Oh, yes. He asked to speak with you straight away. When we told him you were resting, he begged that we let him know the moment you arose. So." Aglaea's grin deepened. "Should we? Or should we keep him stewing?"

Aglaea and Euphrosyne waited, lips peeled in conspiratorial

smiles. Only Thalia hesitated, watching me still, and I loved her for her caution.

If they saw the marks still on my breasts, arm, and cunt through the thin, sheer fabric of the robe, they said nothing. But I felt every mark I had made suddenly, and the rush of making them came back, dizzying me.

"I don't think he needs to stew," I said. "Send for him. I'll receive him now."

Hephaestus was at my door within moments, so abruptly that I knew he must have followed Thalia and Aglaea from summoning him.

I had changed into a loose, simple gown of purest ivory, the pleated fabric hugging my curves and shifting like water as I adjusted and readjusted at the table where I sat with Euphrosyne. We looked up when Thalia slipped in with a startled, "He comes, my lady!"

I rose. I didn't know why my breathing stunted. My legs, arms, extremities suddenly tingled and twitched, either losing feeling or feeling too much. Had I tucked my hair back enough? Should I have let Euphrosyne put more rouge on my lips? This was foolish. I was fumbling—

The moment he stepped inside, I realized I had not wiped off at least the kohl on my arm.

I pivoted, putting that arm away from him, flushing in sudden embarrassment.

He filled the doorway, having to duck slightly to fully emerge before me. He looked like he had been in deep work and only had had time to wipe his face, slick back his black hair before he'd trailed my nymphs. Indeed, he seemed winded, his breaths coming in tight, quick sips he tried to stifle as he scrubbed his palms on the softened leather of his apron.

"Goddess," he said in greeting.

I let a beat pass. The space filled with his eyes on mine, and he didn't dip lower to gaze at my body the way others had. His hands were in fists, though, knuckles white; he was restraining himself in some way.

I waved at the table, the empty chairs. "Please, sit."

"I shouldn't."

I frowned. "My nymphs tell me you came to see me. Not ill tidings, I hope?"

I meant it as a joke.

His lips tugged, and he dragged a hand across his open mouth.

"It may be," he finally said.

My stomach seized. "Oh?"

He took a step forward, his eyes darting to the nymphs. "May we speak in private?"

There was a pleading look in him, one laced with sincerity, that had me nodding at Thalia, Aglaea, and Euphrosyne.

They bowed and slipped into an adjoining room. Thalia lingered last, giving me a heavy stare. "Call for us if you have need of us," she said, with a backwards glare at Hephaestus.

She did not trust him.

And I realized that my trust of him was based on one encounter, one rescue, one sweet conversation. It had been no small thing, but was I wrong to feel this way about him? I did not truly know him.

When we were alone, he held his eyes to mine, though it seemed to take effort. "I must confess something to you. You have not yet heard, have you?"

I cocked my head and let silence be my answer.

"I spoke with Zeus," he said. "I sought a way to . . . extend my claim over you. For your protection only. I thought—" He caught himself, tripping on his words, until his hands fell open at his sides and he shut his eyes in a roll of shame. "My intention backfired. We are to be wed."

His words took a moment to sink in.

"Wed?" I echoed.

He nodded and cut his eyes open to watch me.

I stared at him, waiting for more explanation. When he gave none, I huffed. "How is this a backfire, exactly? What did you intend to do?"

His cheeks, already reddened, flushed deeper. "I thought I could have Zeus declare us married. He has done it in the past; ceremonies are mere formalities. I thought I could convince him to give me that privately, so I might have more solid, lasting claim to you, that you could exist in Olympus without threat or attack for as long as you desired. And then, one day, when you found another, I could have Zeus dissolve it without you needing to know."

My whole face grew wider the more he spoke. I felt as though I had just stumbled from the sea again—newly formed and desperately trying to make sense of things.

"You thought you could marry me in secret? Without even *me* knowing?"

"Yes."

He said it so simply that my body shook and I clamped my arms around my chest to stay the tremble.

"You should have spoken to me of this plan!"

Again, no hesitation. "Yes." His brows pinched in his regret. "Goddess, I cannot express my grief. I never intended for it to go this far—"

"Far? Wait." I pressed the pad of my finger to the skin over my nose, eyes shut, pieces forming.

"We are to be married now," I stated. "In a ceremony?"

"Yes."

"Such as the one with Peleus and Thetis?"

When he didn't answer verbally, I looked up.

He nodded, once.

I felt the blood drain from my face.

All of the gods in attendance had imagined me on that bed. Spread and dripping and theirs to watch—only I would be an even brighter star to them, as captivated as they were with me, and as inexperienced as my body was.

I went immobile. "You should have spoken to me," I echoed feebly.

Hephaestus took a single step forward, his iron boots clanking. Why did he wear those? But my mind didn't stay on them for long.

"Yes, Goddess, yes—I should have spoken to you first," he said, his words coming in a rush. "I was driven mad. It is no excuse, but I have seen firsthand what the other gods do with beautiful things, and I couldn't—"

"I am not a *thing!*" It tore out of me, and that was perhaps the most heartbreaking moment—that this god, whom I had thought to be different, saw me as the same sort of object that the others did.

Hephaestus reeled. "No. You are not a thing." He stepped closer again, and the rage I had first seen in him welled up, striking a harsh color in his cheeks and a simmering light in his eyes. "You are not a thing at all. If you were, I would haul you down to my forge and lock you away so they could never lay a finger on you again. But you are infinitely more, in every way, and this is the only avenue I could think of to protect the magnificence of you from being shattered by the gluttony of them."

My immobility now was not in shock. It was in hypnosis.

Magnificence.

My lips parted, the beat of blood thundering in the tips of my fingers where I had them clamped around my torso.

Hephaestus wilted in the silence that followed. He hovered over me, making me twist my neck up to stare into his eyes, the scent of his skin heady with iron and sweat and so astonishingly masculine that I was frenzied by the sudden need to lick the sheen off his neck, to taste that skin.

I listened to the rush of exhale from him, the wash of inhale into his lungs, until my own breathing calmed enough that I could speak.

"There is no getting out of this?" I whispered.

Hephaestus shook his head. "Not without Ares and Apollo and every other god knowing you are open for the taking."

"And the ceremony. The . . . public consummation. It is set?"

His jaw clamped. He dipped his eyes to the side, shame again—

But his gaze sharpened.

Focused.

He was staring at my arm.

Hephaestus's posture changed utterly, slackened and re-morseful back to that blinding rage in a second flat.

He surged closer and laid his fingers over the smear of black. "Who did this? What—"

His eyes traveled over my body, searching for other marks in a quick sweep.

Embarrassment burned through me. I did not think he would see— I could cover the one on my arm, could lie it away—

But his eyes caught on the outline of my breasts, and I realized how sheer this fabric was, white and pulled taught so the black smears were clearly visible.

His shoulders arched.

I watched a quake start in his fingertips where they barely ghosted over the mark on my arm.

"Who. Did. This?" he repeated, each word a threat, a promise, a plea.

"Because you claimed me?" A hint of offense tinged my question. "Because I am yours, and they should have known better?"

I could play this game, too. I could—

Hephaestus's eyes snapped to mine, locked in a predatory, unspoken command not to speak or look away.

"Because if someone in this accursed mountain hurt you," he told me, a low, rumbling snarl, "then I will haul them back and dump them at your feet and break every bone in their immortal bodies until they mewl for your forgiveness. Now tell me *who did this to you.*"

I could not *think* in the presence of him, his expanse both physical and primeval and I was thoroughly wrapped up in the universe of this god.

"I did," I said. Whispered. Prayed.

He blinked quickly, something in his face resetting, until his rage parted in confusion. "You did this? To yourself?"

His fingers pressed against my arm. He wiped the mark until the kohl transferred to his thumb.

The questioning look he gave made me feel at once reprimanded and shamed—but the apex of my cunt pulsed, shuddering.

I was caught.

In every way.

"I marked myself," I said the words sluggishly, my lips feeling too heavy, "to mimic your touch."

Hephaestus's eyes flared. "To walk Olympus unmolested?"

He sought a simple explanation.

He was giving me an out.

And it was the last thing I wanted.

"At first." I nodded at the mark on my arm. "This one, yes."

His eyes fell again to it.

The muscles in his jaw bulged. After a long beat, his gaze slid to my breasts.

"And these?" he asked, that growl of rage in his throat again.

When others had stared at my body, I had felt their gazes like invasive groping hands—but Hephaestus's was so maddeningly edging that I couldn't draw air, as though every mote of it between us was evaporating.

"These," I started. I let my arms drop from my chest and rested a hand lightly on my mound through the fabric. "I got carried away."

Hephaestus's eyes flew back to mine.

He said nothing for an endless, aching moment, each second of it making the desire in my cunt blaze, wetness leaking down my thighs. I had wanted to feel the fullness while coming—I wanted that, wanted that with *him*—

His fingers snaked around my arm, and he lowered his face towards mine, closing that remaining distance—until his mouth ground against my ear, the scruff of his short beard burning the side of my face.

Then he spoke.

"You will marry me tomorrow," he said, half a question, half a demand.

"Yes," I gasped. "Yes."

"And that will make you mine. Mine to protect, fully, from any else who would seek to harm you."

"Yes."

"But that does not protect you from me, Goddess, does it?"

My heart stopped beating. My lungs caught.

I was hanging by a thread.

"No," I begged.

"And tomorrow," his words darkened, "when all of Olympus demands to watch us consummate, it will be no hapless fucking, no bored penetration. I will bring your body expertly to such screaming bliss that all in this mountain will tremble to at last bear witness to true heaven. This is the game you play, Goddess, by tempting me like this. I am the god of craftsmanship and skill. And I am very, very skilled indeed."

He tore away, stomped through the room, ripped open the door, and left. It slammed in his wake, shuddering in the wall with such force that I felt that shudder straight to my clit.

I dropped to my knees, fighting for breath.

What had I . . .

What had *happened*?

My nymphs ran into the room instantly.

"Goddess!" Thalia cried.

"Are you all right?" Euphrosyne dropped before me, her hands fluttering across my flushed skin.

I nodded. I couldn't speak, throat dry, swollen.

I managed a moan, then, "Yes. Yes, I'm fine. I'm—"

"Here!" Aglaea handed me a cup of wine. "Drink, Goddess—you are pale!"

Was I? I imagined I was far more than pale, disheveled and panting and a mess, brought to this state by his *words*. He had barely touched me.

And tomorrow.

Tomorrow, he would do far more than merely speak to me.

"My lady," Thalia tried. "What . . . what happened?"

I pressed my fingers to my lips. "I am, apparently, betrothed."

And though none of this had been of my choosing, though the consummation awaiting me tomorrow should have rattled me, the only thing that had me reeling was the impossible fact that I did not want to wait so very long.

10

Hephaestus

I had intended to go to the orb room after seeing her—I had not checked in with my mortals in a day at least—but I could barely manage to think coherently enough to redirect my path.

My forge.

My home.

I needed privacy. Now.

I had not felt this unhinged, borderline manic, in centuries. Perhaps ever. It had taken all of my not inconsiderable strength to keep from ripping that gown from her body—that tempting gown, that *teasing* gown, so see-through and thin—and showing her what sorts of marks I would truly leave on the canvas of her skin.

She had marked herself, pretending it was me.

There was no misinterpreting the streaks of black on her breasts. The way she had grabbed her cunt. The fire in her eyes as I had towered over her.

I slammed into my forge and threw myself at my anvil. The ring of the hammer striking a rod of pure lightning echoed in sharp, chaotic bursts—I drove hard against it, body rocking with each strike, sweat pouring, but the focus I sought slipped through my fingers until I hurled the hammer to the ground and tore free my apron, wrenched down my pleated kilt.

Hand to my rock-stiff cock, I bent my head to the wall of the furnace, letting the heat scald me, punish me, as I humped into my clenched fist.

The begging way she had said *Yes, yes,* was an aphrodisiac on its own. But the pure, untainted lust that had been in her eyes was what drove me over the edge in seconds, grunting and moaning at the scorching stone wall as I peeked, my come splashing to the hot stone in a sizzle.

She wanted me. Impossibly. Undeservedly. After what I had done, and even barring who I was, *what* I was, she *wanted* me.

And I would have to share the sight of us together with all of Olympus.

The high of the orgasm came down instantly.

I could not avoid it. There was no escaping this without jeopardizing her, and I was far past the point of even being able to consider her in danger.

So when tomorrow came, I would merely fuck her in such a way that neither of us even knew there were others present.

For me, it would not be hard.

For her?

I had not lied. I was the god of skill, in every way. I did not partake in this particular skill as often as others, but I would channel every learned ability into her pleasure. All of the knowledge I had come to possess of how to bring a body to shattering orgasm had been gathered for this moment.

She was the Goddess of Love, and tomorrow, I would set the standard for worshipping her.

I cleaned the wall, righted my kilt, and snatched my apron from the floor. My eyes cast around my home, seeing it anew. The main room was my forge, the walls, floor, and ceiling nothing more than jet black chiseled stone—I had never refined it, what with how damaging my work could be. A few rooms branched off: my bedchamber, some scattered storage.

She would likely want to stay in her suite. Few married couples in Olympus lived together. But I would make a space for her, here, if she gave me the honor of coming to my home.

I wanted her to know she was welcome.

I wanted her to know that this was not idle for me. That I had forced us into this, stupidly; but I was not taking it lightly.

I went first to my bedroom. Paused at the door.

Too presumptuous, even for this feverish hope that was roiling in me.

I spent the next hour hauling out extra tools and materials until a separate room was cleared. Building a bed for her was not hard—a few pieces of sturdy oak, hewn already. I had extra blankets and bedding, and the mattress I took from my own bed. Next to it, I set a table, dragged in an empty chest where she might store her things.

Hands on my hips, I surveyed the space under the magic white light that hung from the stone ceiling.

This room was dull and dim and wholly unworthy of her. She was the Goddess of *Beauty*, and this place was all dingy and soot-smeared.

I shoved back out into my forge and sorted through a cabinet where I kept the finest materials. I did not often use these things—mostly my tasks were in weaponry, but the gods and goddesses had once begged me to craft jewelry enchanted with love spells for their flings. It had been decades since I had done such a thing—but were these supplies out of order? I had organized everything, but I did not remember the silver pieces being so close to the rubies, nor did I think I had been so low on gold? And the finer enchantment powder I used in this work looked less than I remembered it too.

No matter. I grabbed handfuls of opals, of diamonds, of deep blue sapphires, and I hauled over my jewelry making table.

I fell into the work, toppled down headfirst. Despite the horrors that haunted Olympus, this had ever been my utopia—the act of creation, of prying something useful or beautiful or masterful from the rubble of our flawed existences.

So when I was done, I stood up, body settled with rightness.

The light-catcher was delicate, each jewel set in a circle of silver, the colors and thinness of the materials meant to allow the faux light to pass through.

I hung it in her room, just over the bed, and stepped back.

A spray of ivory, rainbow hues, and heavy blue danced across the room, giving much-needed glitters of light and color.

It wasn't perfect.

It wasn't enough.

My hands clenched and unclenched and I felt myself on the edge of diving back to my workstation when a heavy knock thundered on my forge's door.

I crossed and yanked it open, a snarl on my lips at being disturbed.

But there stood Zeus. Ares with him.

The muscles in my shoulders turned to iron. "What?"

Zeus's eyebrows rose sardonically. "That is how you greet me?"

"My apologies." *Yes,* I wanted to say. *After what you force me to do tomorrow to that perfect goddess you are unworthy of even being near?*

"Calm, Hephaestus; we do not come to discuss the matter further," said Zeus.

But by the way Ares rolled his eyes, I could tell he had hoped.

"What, then?" I asked.

"There is war on Earth," Ares said. A spark of eagerness lit on his face.

The only thing my brother loved more than conquering was the temptation of a fresh thing to dominate.

I did not let my relief show. Maybe this would draw his attention away from Aphrodite.

"You need weapons? Armor?"

Zeus nodded. "Bolts, too."

I ducked into the forge and set about gathering what they would need. The two followed me in, along with half a dozen nymph servants, and they began listing what specifically they wanted—some of the nets that encased victims to immobility; a new enchanted helmet that allowed flight; a set of bracers that gave extra defense against arrows—and I was glad for this new distraction. This normalcy, I could handle.

I stacked the last of the items into a cart that the servants began to wheel out. "What is the nature of this war?"

Ares's grin was cold. "Greece marches on Troy."

That made me pause. "Troy has long been able to hold off any foe. Why does Greece feel they can change that now?"

"A Trojan prince made off with the Greek king's wife." Ares held my eyes as he spoke. "Greece believes they will use revenge to tear down Troy's mighty walls. But Troy is infinitely more powerful. What Greece cannot keep hold of, Troy won effortlessly."

The tendons in my neck stiffened. My hand fisted on the

edge of my workstation.

"You fight for Troy, then?" I guessed.

"The Greek king believed he won the prize. Troy absconded with it, as is their right." Ares leered at me. "Yes, I fight for Troy. And when I return from battle, victorious, I will abscond with your own prize, Hephaestus. This war between us is not over."

My lip flickered, a barely restrained snarl, and I would have heaved a handful of burning coals at him had Zeus not stepped between us.

"Save the brawls for Earth, Ares," he chuckled.

"Yes," I snapped. "Try hard not to get distracted, God of War, knowing you march into a mortals' conflict on the back of a fresh loss."

Ares lunged, fist wound, and I let his knuckles crack into my jaw.

Pain flared, immediately tempering against the might of my god blood, but I held in the position it threw me, head to the side.

I should not have played into his game. I should not have responded at all.

She was not a *prize*, not something be won or fought over.

"Be glad I will miss your sham of a ceremony tomorrow, brother," Ares snarled at me. "I give you that single moment to screw her. Consider it a wedding gift. But know that what you have once will be the very place I lodge my cock over, and over, and over to exhaustion when I return."

"We have everything," Zeus said, half bored. "Come, Ares."

I was a statue, even my breath stopped, until Ares patted my cheek, and left.

Zeus held by the door. "You may have reached too high with

this one. Do not be surprised when he steals her from you."

"He won't," I stated. Head still to the side. Eyes seeing only red, hot, angry pulses of it.

"Hm. Don't be a fool, Hephaestus. She is not one that can be kept to a single lover."

"Even if she chooses it?" I swung my glare to him. To watch his expression.

Zeus's brows knotted. For once, he looked thoroughly bewildered.

"What does choice have to do with it? She is the Goddess of Love. She was created to be used in this way. Do not deny her nature."

"You know nothing of her nature."

"And you do?" Zeus sighed. "This grows tiresome. I must see off those who leave for the war."

He walked out, leaving the door open in his wake, until I watched his form vanish up a set of stairs.

The protection of my marriage to Aphrodite would hold only as long as Zeus's good graces. If he decided he wanted her? If he grew angry with me? He could rip her away with the flick of his wrist. I relied on this protection only in so far as the other gods feared disobeying Zeus's commands. But if Zeus himself rescinded it?

What then?

I was a fool. I had let myself be so distracted by *her*, by the magic of her, that I had gone to an extreme in error. And though it was too late to undo it, I had other solutions at my fingertips. Quite literally.

I had just piled high a cart of enchanted weapons and armor.

I tore through my materials. Gold, silver, the finest I could find—I spread it over my workstation, readying it, that manic frenzy returning, but driven by the lingering stench of Zeus and Ares in my home.

And so I set about sculpting one more thing for Aphrodite.

One enchanted gift that would protect her if, horrifically, I could not.

11

Aphrodite

I rose the next morning to the excited twittering of my nymphs.

"Come, Goddess!" Aglaea took my wrist from beneath the soft bedding. "We have displayed gowns for you to choose from. We must get you ready!"

"For your *wedding!*" Euphrosyne giggled.

I eyed them, my smile cautious.

I had barely slept at all last night. Not that that was unusual, Thalia had assured me when she had found me pacing the room. But even after hours—*hours*—of rolling every detail in my mind, I still had not decided how I should feel today.

A wedding seemed like it should be cause for rejoicing. But what I had seen of Peleus and Thetis's wedding was ludicrous. And the one awaiting me today would be transactional only—save for the way my body ached to be near Hephaestus again. His words had left a satiny texture on my skin and when I had not been pacing last night, I had been under the blankets, fingers in my cunt, moans stifled into the pillows.

He would fuck me in full view of Olympus today. In full

view of Ares.

I kept telling myself that, and waiting for the back blow of horror.

It never came.

And so I let the nymphs pull me into a warm bath, where at last I scrubbed off the marks of kohl. Today, so shortly, Hephaestus's actual hands would be on these places I had imagined.

I flushed, and it had nothing to do with the heat of the bath.

When I was dressed, seated before the mirror so Euphrosyne could style my hair, my door opened.

No knock. No courtesy.

So I knew immediately who it was, and the hairs along my arms stood at end.

Ares pushed into the doorway, casting his eyes around. He spent a long moment staring at my reflection, studying my face for any tells.

And I was not good at hiding those tells from him. So I know he saw the line my lips made, the flinch when he stepped inside.

"Leave," I told him. "I am occupied."

"Ah, yes. Preparing yourself to be a monster's cock warmer."

I snapped my eyes away from the reflection of his.

But I heard his steps thud closer.

Euphrosyne bowed and ducked away at his approach. Aglaea, on a chaise sorting through necklaces, kept her head down.

Only Thalia stood strong, coming close to put her hand on my shoulder. "My lady asked you to—"

"Fuck off, nymph."

I gaped up at Ares. "Do not speak to her like that!"

His head tipped, seeming honestly confused about why I was upset. "I'll speak to her however I like." He studied her more closely. "Haven't I had you before? So yes, I will address her as any other bitch."

My eyes caught Thalia's in the mirror. She had as good as said she'd slept with him, and I knew in that moment that it had been under much the same situation as when Ares had assaulted me. Only she had shrugged it off, saying *We are nymphs*, as though that softened it.

Had I been the one to make her realize the invasion of it? Was I the reason her eyes teared and she looked, now, brittle?

I shot up from the bench. "Leave. Take your arrogance and *leave*, Ares."

"But I have a wedding gift for you, and I won't be able to give it to you at the celebration."

"I want nothing from you."

He held up a necklace. It was simple, a chain holding a small gold coin emblazoned with two serpents, each eating the other's tale. And while it would have been lovely, from his hands, it was hideous.

"A gift of beauty for the Goddess of Beauty," Ares said.

I did not accept it.

After a drawn-out moment of rival pride where he waited for me to take it and I refused to even face him, finally, it was Thalia who accepted the necklace. "She thanks you, God Ares," she murmured.

"Does she?" Ares sneered at my reflection.

"Why could this not have waited for the celebration? For future, you are forbidden from coming to my suite unless summoned."

"Ah, is that so? Well, Beauty, something tells me you will be summoning me. Although not for days at least, I'm afraid."

I squinted at him. "Days? Never."

"*Days* because I regret to say that I have been called away."

I went still.

Ares stepped closer, closer, until his breastplate pressed to my bare arm, his breath beating down on the side of my face. "War summons from Earth. I know you must endure this wedding, but at least try to think of me when he's fumbling around your cunt."

I whirled away. Ares caught my arm, and the echo of his touch from Peleus and Thetis's wedding sent a jarring ripple through me, so even though I was livid, even though I *burned* with hatred for his mere presence, I went utterly, appallingly immobile.

He drew me closer, and I walked, stumbling, terror washing through me.

"I am not a plaything," I managed to say. "Release me."

"Aren't you?" Ares ignored my plea. His eyes roamed my body, the gown I had chosen—gold with a plunging neckline, an overlay of sheer fabric set with crystal beads that sparkled like stars. "Look at you, Beauty. You're walking sex. Why do you fight it so hard?"

I dropped my weight into my heels, pulling at the unyielding grip of him. "Let me *go*—"

A presence appeared behind Ares. When had he entered the room? I hadn't heard, hadn't noticed, but suddenly, Hephaestus was here.

"Get your hands," he started, "off my betrothed."

Ares twitched around.

He said nothing. Only stared at Hephaestus, his grip tightening, tightening on my wrist, until I began to buckle, mouth opening in a soundless whimper.

Why could our immortal bodies feel pain at all? Why were

we capable of this horrifying sensation?

Ares released me.

I noticed, then, the axe in Hephaestus's hand, wicked and curved, the blade poised at Ares's throat.

"Enjoy her while you can," Ares said to Hephaestus.

He left, casting me one final leer.

I rushed after him and slammed the door, my limbs shaking, breath stunted.

And then, because my own reaction of immobility had shattered me, I hurled myself onto Hephaestus.

He bent down to catch me, his axe dropping in a startled clatter on the marble floor. "Did he hurt you? Are you—"

I buried my face in his neck, in the curve of skin I had wanted yesterday to taste. He was a wall of muscle, the whole wide girth of him, and the direct contact of being in his arms tapped a whimper from my throat.

"Thank you," I told him. Again. I would be thanking him daily. How was this a life?

I shook, and I felt his hand rub my back.

"It is our arrangement," he said. His voice was thick. "And I have brought something else in that vein."

That pulled me from his arms. My eyes were blurry—I wasn't quite crying, but I was tousled in every way.

He had cleaned up for our wedding. No leather apron, no soot-streaks. His hair was styled back across his head and his beard was trimmed and neat against the flame-touched brown to his skin. He wore a fine silk toga and a thick brown belt and he smelled of spiced soap, but beneath it lay still that scent of him, iron and masculinity that now had my fear unwinding, thread by thread.

Hephaestus watched my face for a moment. I saw the

emotions pass over him—rage, bright and beautiful; regret; concern.

But he managed a small, gentle smile. "Here."

He extended something he unhooked from his belt.

It was a strophion, a sort of crisscrossing band I had seen in my supply of clothes. This one was the finest yet, made of braided strands of gold and silver and other metals, set with gems in varying shades of teal and blue. The band made an X that would cross directly between my breasts when worn.

I took it, the breath bursting out of me. "It's stunning." I looked up at him. "I have no gift for you!"

His eyelids fluttered.

Then he laughed.

It was so brief, the gentlest flash of humor, but it caught me up in a windstorm.

"This is no mere wedding gift, Goddess," he said. "It is a further way I can protect you. This band," he laid a finger on the edge, "is enchanted so that when you wear it, only those you wish may touch you. The rest receive . . . incentive not to do so again."

"Incentive?"

"They'll be struck by lightning. Mildly. Some risk of unconsciousness."

I stared at him. Stared and stared.

Then I, too, laughed.

The tears I had been fighting trickled free, born on relief, and I held the strophion to my chest. "Thank you. How did you make this?"

"I create enchanted weapons regularly." He winced. "I should have thought of this solution sooner. I should have thought of it first. I am sorry, again, Goddess. I—"

"Aphrodite," I corrected.

He held. Though it seemed to take effort, "Aphrodite. I am sorry."

"You have done more to help me than anyone here yet," I told him, wilted in honest truth. "Do not apologize. I owe you . . . so much."

Hephaestus's cheeks darkened. "I would ask one thing of you."

"Name it." I should not have been so eager, maybe. But I could not help it. I still felt the heat of him on my arms, on my chest.

He lowered his hand to his side, the strophion rocking in my grip. "Wear this today."

My brows furrowed.

"Wear it," he licked his lip, "so Olympus will see it as a warning of what protects you now."

His request took a beat to connect fully in my mind.

He thought that if I wore this strophion to our wedding, during our consummation, that it would strike him with lightning. That all would see it reject him because I had rejected him, and they would be warned against the power I had now.

With this creation in my hands, I finally decided how I should feel about today.

Ares would not be there.

Hephaestus had given me a level of protection that was dependent on my own choices, not on his claim.

"All right," I agreed. "I will wear it."

His breath caught. He gathered himself and nodded, confirmation, before he turned to leave.

"But it will not work on you," I added.

He stopped.

I watched the muscles in his back tense through the silk, seeing every line, the valleys and hills of a body sculpted not by divine magic, but by physical labor.

Hephaestus glanced back. Just once.

There was pure heat in his gaze, molten fire that I felt sizzle across the space between us.

"You may say so," he told me. "But we will see what your body truly decides, won't we?"

As he had left before, he stormed from the room, and I knew now it was because he was on the edge of the same precipice where I balanced, teetered, wanting to fall.

The moment he was gone, Thalia surged towards me, that necklace from Ares still in her hand. "My lady! What—"

But her words failed. She stared at the strophion, and the look that passed over her face was an echo of Olympus's hunger, but a fragile, reverent sort of wanting. The tears that had been in her eyes gathered again, welling.

All my interactions with my nymphs crashed back on me, along with the concern I had felt in the orgy, in wondering who in the room was being used against their will—I felt a solution, here in the palm of my hands.

Did Hephaestus realize how mighty a tool he had made? Something like this could alter the darkest element of Olympus I had come across.

This could change everything.

I dipped my head to get Thalia's attention. "I will have him make one for you. For all of you."

Thalia gaped at me. "Truly, Goddess?"

"He will be my husband. I will see it done."

Thalia bit her lip. She looked back at Aglaea and Euphrosyne, shocked and stationary on the chaise, and the three of them shared another unspoken conversation, lifted eyebrows and pleading looks.

"We are honored to be yours, Goddess," Thalia said finally. "Honored, truly."

12

Hephaestus

I had never cared much for how celebrations on Olympus came together. Why should I have? Refreshments appeared, decorations manifested; whether through magic or servant, did it matter?

It did.

She was making me see that.

If only because the moment I stepped into the banquet hall, none of these decorations were good enough.

My jaw tightened. There was no time to correct anything, and so I glared at each tuft of pink flowers and the trays of sugared dates as though they could bear the brunt of my churning emotions.

She did not think the strophion would work on me.

I walked, adjusting my tunic, hating that I had not worn armor or my apron or something to better cover the swelling of my cock.

Regardless of what she said—regardless of what my cock was saying—I hoped the strophion would work on me. Nothing would send a message through the gods more effectively than one of their own getting laid out flat by a blast of lightning. I had triggered it to even effect Zeus, God of Lightning, should he take liberties. The jarring crash of reminding all present that we could, in fact, feel *pain*, and that Aphrodite now was capable of inflicting that, would guarantee her safety more than anything else I could do.

But if the strophion did not work when I touched her.

If she left me lay her down on the marital bed and run my hands up her soft thighs and—

I walked, pacing the room, as it began to fill. The guests avoided me, whether from my reputation or the menacing way I glowered at each of them. My cock was hard to the point of pain and I was not sure how I would get through this feast, this celebration, this *day*.

Music started. That, at least, was befitting her, a gentle warble of harps.

As if cued by it, she appeared in the doorway.

I made for her instantly, a rumble in my chest. *Mine. Mine to protect.*

With Ares in her room, I had barely had time to admire how she had chosen to appear for our wedding. Her gold dress was sumptuous, highlighting each perfect curve, a slit up the side revealing her leg as she walked; and the sheer drape of jewel-dotted mesh over top showed the long, teasing gap between her breasts, the skin beneath dusted with powder that glittered in the faux sun. Beyond her clothing, designed to purposefully drive me wild, her gold-lined eyes were bright and fixed on me, her full lips painted wine-red and lifting in a smile.

She wore the strophion over everything, the braided metal strands crisscrossing between her breasts and making them stick out more, and I realized, with a jolt of panic and hot need, that I had given her a gift that made her body even more desirable.

Mine, the word echoed, but it receded into awe. Startled, worship-driven awe.

I stopped in front of her, loomed closer than I had previously dared. The feel of her body when she had jumped into my arms made my fingers twitch to grab her again, and the way the strophion emphasized her breasts did not help.

"Thank you again," she whispered and touched the strophion. "I do not think you know what a gift you have given."

I did, though. I did in ways that shamed me to silence, that I had been so stupid as to not even consider a creation like this until her.

So brief her time had been on Olympus, and already, she was changing things utterly.

"You are most welcome, Goddess," I said softly.

I could feel the whole of the room look at her. Staring. Soaking in the sight of her, gold-clad and voluptuous.

Her eyes lifted to mine and she gave the quietest of gasps, and I felt the way I was watching her now, voracious. Like I was envisioning slamming her into the wall and sheathing myself in her.

I was.

Vividly.

And she smiled.

I shook myself back.

"The crowd is smaller," she noted, focus flashing around us.

"Yes. Yes." I scratched my chin, mind fighting to steady. "The war has called many away. To our benefit—the consummation will be less attended."

"A relief," she said. Did she sound truly relieved? Was there a hitch in her voice, a pause? "What is the war? Why is it important?"

"Greece and Troy have long been thorns in the other's side," I said. "Greece finally made a move. Well, I suppose Troy did—a Trojan prince stole the Greek king's wife."

Her head tipped, the sheen of her black hair lustrous. "And that caused a war?"

"Greece's Queen Helen is proclaimed to be the most beautiful mortal to—"

"Helen?"

"Yes. Helen."

Aphrodite's eyes widened. She had been listening with interest before; now she stared in growing concern. "The Trojan prince is not Paris, is he?"

I nodded.

She lifted a hand to her lips.

Immediately, I drew closer to her, creating a shield of my body around her. "What is wrong? How do you know these mortals?"

"I gave them that gift," she said, panting. "I blessed them with enduring love. I did not know— I did not realize she was married to another— Their love seemed so pure!"

"It is all right. You cannot think—"

"Did I cause a war?"

Her wide, round eyes peeked up at me, a mortifying innocence in her question.

It resonated, each word, each second of genuine concern.

Never, in the history of my time on Olympus, had any other god expressed such honest worry over mortals.

I clasped my hands at my sides, tremors begging me to swoop her up, to hold her in comfort; to drop to my knees and revel in her mere presence.

How had such a being come to be here, in this place of frivolity and selfishness? And yet here she was, and here I was, and I knew, in that moment, that I had irrevocably fallen in love with her.

"After the wedding," I said, "I will take you to the orb room, so you may check in on them."

"Thank you. Yes." She wilted, shoulders burdened.

"Do not take the weight of their war," I pleaded. "Mortals find any cause they can to kill each other. What you did in giving Paris and Helen their love—it was one bright spot of beauty in a world otherwise beset by the same greed you see here. You did, can only do, good, Goddess."

The strain around her eyes relaxed, lashes fluttering. "How many times must I bid you call me Aphrodite?"

I leaned down, not touching her, my lips so close to her ear that I could smell the perfume the nymphs had padded against her neck—vanilla, sweet and warming.

"I call you Goddess," I whispered, "to keep myself in check about what you are. If I called you Aphrodite, I would only be able to think of the whined, begging way you said you would marry me."

Her breath halted. I swore I could feel the quickening of her pulse palpitating the air between us.

"So after we are wed, you will call me Aphrodite?"

"Yes."

"How often?"

"Every day. Every hour. Every moment you allow me to."

"Hephaestus."

The first she had truly said my name, and it was breathy with need.

My cock surged to full hardness, precum trickling out, dampening my tunic. I bit down, hard, jaw shatteringly tight, to stop from coming right there.

Her eyes lowered. She saw my erection. I did not try to hide it—she needed to know what she did to me, that I was not words alone, that my body was attuned to her now, hers in every growing way.

And every piece of this body that was now hers cried out in irreversible ecstasy as I watched her hand reach down, fingers stretching towards my cock—

"Aphrodite!"

The cry cut into me with a gut-wrenching yank back to reality, and I spun away, air bursting through my nose as I faced the wall.

"Oh—um, Demeter, yes?" Aphrodite said to the invader. Her voice trembled with the retreating quakes of desire venting, unfulfilled.

Demeter's squawking voice exclaimed over her loveliness, asking questions of her time here so far but not pausing long enough for Aphrodite to answer; and I used these seconds to press into the frame of the nearby door, coming down from the ache of that singular moment deflating.

This was but a precursor to what the consummation would be. The two of us falling into each other, only to be jarringly ripped apart by a whistle, a filthy shout.

I would put every modicum of my abilities into making sure she not only enjoyed herself, but had an experience unmatched. But no matter what I did, the other gods would be there.

Like these decorations, the food, it was not good enough for her.

Finally, my cock had softened enough that I could turn

began to fear it was cursed to be in a state of half-hardness until I felt her touch, but through an effort of primal strength, I came up behind Aphrodite.

Demeter prattled on about how she would have to introduce Aphrodite to her daughter. "Persephone is so like you!" Demeter said. "So . . . spirited."

From her, it was not a compliment.

I let my presence alongside Aphrodite be contact enough. She swayed closer to me, her eyes lifting to mine, and my hand burned to touch the small of her back, to guide her away.

But I would not touch her yet. I would not let the strophion have its effect until—

Apollo sauntered over.

Demeter gave him a dull stare. "Apollo. You do not go to war?"

"Not yet." He shrugged. "I'll let Ares take the first blood. My glory will come later."

Unsurprising. The God of the Sun cared less for these conflicts than Ares, even if Troy worshipped him most of all.

I surveyed the rest of those in attendance. Zeus was not yet here. Why did he drag it out? His overbearing need to make a dramatic appearance . . .

Aphrodite flinched suddenly, and I took stock of our situation with a predator's sweep.

Apollo had moved closer. He made her uncomfortable.

I flashed him a tight warning glare.

He frowned. "What's that about?" He hooked an arm around Demeter. "On your wedding day, and can't even manage a smile, eh, monster?"

"Do not call him that," snapped Aphrodite.

My eyes widened down at her. Demeter and Apollo both

seemed briefly stunned.

No one . . . *defended* me. I had long grown accustomed to their insults. I was the lone deformed god in a heaven of perfection.

I felt the weight of my iron boots, the way Demeter glanced at them and quickly away.

Apollo laughed, loud and bellowing, dragging the attention of the room to us.

"You are the Goddess of Beauty, but also of *delusion*," he scoffed. "Don't tell me we didn't have fun at the last wedding!"

"No. I did not." Aphrodite's tone was ice.

I tipped down to her. The energy beating off of her coiled rage in my chest. "What did he do?"

I had not noted where he had been during Thetis and Peleus's wedding. She had been on Ares's lap—where had Apollo been? Likely nearby, ever chasing Ares's fun.

What had he done to her?

Her jaw clamped and she twisted half towards me—

"Oh, come now, Aphrodite!" Apollo leaned forward, tugging Demeter with him, who winced and scowled at him. "I know you liked *this*."

And he reached out and pinched her breast.

My vision went red.

I had brought no weapons, stupidly, but in this moment, I was the deadliest weapon in the mountain.

But I did not get a moment to move before a sizzling lightning bolt flared out of Aphrodite's strophion and blasted Apollo across the room.

The whole of the banquet hall went perfectly immobile.

The music stopped playing. Every god, demigod, nymph, and servant stared at the God of the Sun as he staggeringly picked himself up from the marble floor, his toga singed black, revealing a slowly healing burn in the center of his chest.

Sweat poured down his face and he gaped across the room at Aphrodite, first in fear, then in a tight swell of offended horror.

Where Ares would have raged, and likely done something to get electrocuted again, Apollo simply trudged off, holding his chest, a beaten, sad retreat.

The moment he left the room, Aphrodite cut a fuming gaze around. "Let that be the only warning I will give," she declared.

Her words were immovably solid, but I saw a tremble in her hands, at the edge of her lips.

"Goddess," I whispered to her. "Goddess—"

She looked up at me. That look was connection enough, here in this too-public place, and again, I was only able to resist holding her due to the fact that she had not initiated it, she had not asked. I could not assume. Would not assume. I was aching to comfort her, but I stood as close as I dared, waiting, waiting, waiting.

"Where is Zeus?" she asked, winded.

"Let us find him," I said.

She nodded and set off, pushing past an utterly speechless Demeter.

We had gotten a few paces only when Zeus's trumpets rang. His parade of servants trailed in ahead of him through the archway at the far end, and as he entered, he immediately noted the attitude of the room, that heavy, incorrigible shock.

"What sort of celebration do you throw, Hephaestus?" Zeus bellowed, trying for good-natured. But I could see the twinge of concern in him.

"A wedding, of course," I said as Aphrodite and I neared him. "Let it be done."

His eyes narrowed, flicking between us. "No pretense, hm?"

"Is there ever any here?"

"You think so little of us, Hephaestus. It pains me."

My very existence beneath you pains me. "On with it."

Zeus sighed. He gauged the room again, still unsure of the source of the tension, but he would soon be told, I knew. Apollo would run to him and complain. Nothing would happen—I knew how little repercussion came. The only justice lay in that which we could grab ourselves.

"Fine." Zeus held his hands over Aphrodite and I, palms down. "Hephaestus and Aphrodite. Do you submit to being wed as husband and wife before Zeus, King of Gods, Ruler of Olympus and All Beings Below?"

"I do," I said instantly. Forcefully. I still teetered on the edge of fury and denied release, a wound thing winding tighter. I barely heard myself.

I wanted to get her out of here.

I wanted to ask if I could touch her, to list all the reasons why I should—and shouldn't—be given that honor, and let her decide.

But then Aphrodite lifted her chin. "I do as well," she said, and there wasn't the slightest tremor in her voice.

Zeus nodded. "By my powers, I declare it so. Hephaestus and Aphrodite are wed."

There was no applause, on pomp.

Zeus started to turn to grab a goblet a wine from a nearby servant. I released a breath, doing a quick sweep of my internal fortifications—how much strength would I need to hold myself against the time between now and the time when Zeus called for the consummation? Would I—

But Aphrodite hadn't moved. "Let it begin," she declared.

Zeus swung his head back to look at her. Calculation passed over his face, nothing menacing; fascination, almost, or surprise. He liked being surprised, when it benefitted him.

And she was asking to begin the consummation.

Now.

My whole body rocked, eyes bulging wide as I stared at the side of her face, but she was looking at Zeus.

Her hand balled into a fist. Relaxed. Tightened again.

"Eager, are you?" Zeus gave a lascivious grin. "Very well. It is the bride's day, after all."

He began walking through the crowd, towards the corner where the bed would appear, where servants were now in a frantic scramble to arrange chaises and chairs.

I stayed rooted next to Aphrodite. Who still did not look up at me.

"Aphrodite." I hated the way I said her name, a reveal of all the roiling regret that thudded in me, that I was forcing her to do this, that *I* had been the cause of this—

But she looked up at me. Her eyes were glistening, and I knew she was afraid; but there was a glimmer in her too, a spark of desire that had not waned, that was growing stronger.

"I want you, Hephaestus," she told me. "I want you."

It was too impossible a thing for her to say.

How, *how*, could something like me deserve her? But I didn't, I would never, and yet she was telling me she wanted me anyway.

"You want me," I echoed, feeling the weight of that fact. "Do you want this?"

I nodded towards the gathering crowd.

Her eyes did not leave mine and she hesitated so slightly that I had my answer.

"But you will be there," she said. "It will be you, and that is what I want."

Her words dipped. *It will be you.*

There was something more beneath that phrase. An intention that had my eyes narrowing, studying her face.

And then I realized.

I realized.

As though her strophion had pelted me with a bolt of lightning.

I rocked backwards, tearing a hand through my hair, dread painting me in all wide features. "You are a virgin."

I had not thought I could feel more horrified at what I had forced her to.

I had not thought I could feel more of an idiot than I was.

Of course she was a virgin. I had *watched her creation* only days ago. But the very *existence* of a virgin on Olympus was such a rare, incredible feat that even seeing her newly-formed body, I had not registered that as part of her. In that way, I was like Ares, like Apollo, like all who had sought to immediately use her.

My breath came in tight, hitched gasps. "I am so sorry. This is unforgiveable, that I did not realize—Goddess, I—"

She stepped closer to me. "Hephaestus, it's all right. You are my one ally here."

"And a poor, stupid ally at that."

She smiled. How could she? And yet I took it, grabbed onto it. She was capable of smiling, so she was not as brittle as I was fearing.

I said that to myself again—*she is not brittle. It is my own fear that is brittle.*

She is stronger than I could ever be.

And this—displayed before all of Olympus like a feast they could tear apart with their teeth—would *not* be her first time. Not with me. Not for *her*.

"Do you trust me?" I whispered.

The crowd had gathered. Musicians began playing again, a low, pulsing melody.

Aphrodite nodded without hesitation.

I loved this goddess. I loved her, and I did not deserve her, and I would do everything in my power from here on out to be worthy of her.

"Then come, and do as I say," I told her, and I walked towards the bed.

13

Aphrodite

I followed Hephaestus across the room. We wove through the arranged crowd—less packed than before, and that fact alone alleviated a large part of my anxiety.

But each step we took closer to the bed, my arms shook, the shift of my gown against my skin rubbing sensitivity directly to my clit.

I focused on Hephaestus's back. The cut of his muscles through his tunic. The memory of his stiff cock lifting between us, and the knowledge that he had not touched me, even with how hard I had made him.

I was so wound for him that a large part of me wanted nothing more than to shove him onto the bed and give him my body, see what he would do with it.

But the eyes that flashed to me were instantly grating. Zeus, and others, names I knew but couldn't call up; all I could feel was that hunger burning in them, tainted now by what they had seen my strophion do. Or did they think it was me, somehow? Either way, they watched me with greedy hunger tinged with malice. They wanted to see me brought low—I had harmed one of them. One of us.

The fact that Apollo had harmed me first, that he had insisted on grabbing me as he had when Ares had held me as an offering to him, did not seem to matter.

My own anger itched deep, disgust building at these creatures I was forced to reign alongside.

So I kept my focus on Hephaestus. Just Hephaestus.

How had I come to find him here, impossibly, in this den of greed? The one true source of gentleness and goodness, and he stopped at the bed and looked back at me, and I knew he would see me through this. I knew whatever he told me to do, I would, and it would not only appease the vicious beasts around us, but would speak to the desire that still ached in me for him.

The music trilled. Glasses clinked. No one had begun fucking yet, all eyes pinned on me.

I stopped in front of Hephaestus, close enough to breathe the scent of him, and all he did was untie his belt.

It dropped to the floor with a heavy thunk.

He grabbed the edge of his tunic and hefted it over his body, the powerful muscles of his torso stretching and contorting with his arms over his head, and that quickly, he was naked, keeping on only his iron boots.

I could not form a single coherent thought.

The dark hair of his beard curled across his broad, chiseled chest, the tight plane of his stomach, and down, bending in an arrow-straight line between a dipped V in the muscles of his pelvis. That line fed to his cock, erect and hard between his massive thighs.

All my daydreams of using my fingers to feel him in my cunt were woeful.

The *size* of him.

Not merely long, but thick, a rod marbled with swollen purple veins, the hole at the tip glistening.

My mouth watered, and I again wanted to taste him—but to taste *that* specifically, to lap the moisture at the tip.

"Aphrodite," he said.

I couldn't move. My body had forgotten all its functions save for my cunt throbbing, an emptiness that was swallowing me whole.

Finally, I managed to look up at his eyes, seeing the flush across his cheeks, that blush now spreading down his chest. I knew I was wholly aflame, every piece of me red with exertion and the desperation of desire, and he had not even touched me.

He had not *touched me*, and I had not touched *him*, and that was the greatest sin in this entire mountain.

Hephaestus reached for me.

He hesitated.

I nodded, so subtly, barely a motion at all.

His reach continued, stretching, until his beefy hand took my wrist.

The strophion did not react.

I would have torn it from my body if it had.

A murmur rippled through the crowd. I felt their greed twist—*why him? Why does she allow him?*

"I told you it wouldn't work on you," I whispered, all stunted breath.

I lifted the hand he held to press my palm flat on the center of his chest, the exact spot where my strophion had blasted into Apollo.

"Do you give me permission, Goddess?" he asked.

I nodded. My hair shook into my face.

I wanted to beg him. To whine my need.

His face hardened. He glanced to the side. To Zeus.

"Your permission most of all," he said, disgust ripe in his tone. "God-King."

I remembered the way Thetis had been flushed with longing, riled by Peleus before Zeus had agreed. I did not have to fake the way I was desperate for Hephaestus, but I could not bring myself to look at Zeus, Hephaestus the center of my world.

Zeus gave a chuckle. "You'd better before she comes un-touched."

Laughs went around. I could not even feel shamed—yes, this virile god had driven me to such desire; let them know that.

Hephaestus backed onto the bed and sat. "Aphrodite." His voice went soft again. "Spread your legs around me."

The way he said even that was a cacophony of intimacy, the rattling cap on the building pressure of his control.

I stepped forward, obedience my only guide.

"Undress her!" someone called.

A chorus of whoops and agreement.

Hephaestus didn't look away from me. He wetted his lips, and I was fixated on the sheen there.

"You will never take this off with others present." His words were low, just for me, as he hooked one finger into the strophion. "Only with me, alone."

"Yes," I said.

"Trust me, Goddess," he said again, and he began to lift the skirt of my gown.

The crowd cheered. My heart had been racing already, but it somehow found the drive to go faster.

Hephaestus did not undress me. He merely hefted my skirt

to the middle of my thighs and gently prodded me closer to him.

I steadied with a hand on his shoulder and lifted first one knee on the bed, the silk soft next to his thigh, then the other, until I straddled him. My dripping cunt floated over his cock as he let the skirt fall, the heat between us trapped beneath my gown and scorching to unbearable heights.

I hovered above his face, holding onto his neck like an anchor, staring down into his glistening, dark eyes.

He tucked one hand beneath my skirt.

I hissed air through my nose, expecting him to position himself at my opening. *Yes*, I wanted to say, and also *No*, a crash of contradiction—not here, not with these eyes on us—

But he did not enter me.

He flattened his hardness to his stomach and pulled me to sit on his thighs, his cock pinned between us. The bulk of it dragged on my clit as I lowered down, and that contact, minimal though it was, sparked a more powerful electrocution than my strophion.

My eyes rolled back, my mouth parted, a soft, small cry escaping me.

"Is she tight?" a voice called.

"Undress her!" again. "Show us what you claimed, Hephaestus!"

They were fading more and more to the background.

I bent double over him, slowly losing control. Having his raw cock against my cunt, feeling the shudder and shiver of his massive body beneath me, him naked, me fully clothed—it was so unraveling, in the greatest, most monumental way, that I scrambled through the air until I found his mouth with my own.

I barely heard the gasp that surged through the crowd.

Barely felt the shift in the attitude—from eagerly watching me get fucked, to awkward cringes of them knowing they now witnessed something intimate.

The pinpoint of my existence whittled down to this god's lips on mine. His mouth held open for a singular beat, letting me explore him—a lick at his tongue, the taste of spice in him, heat and velvet.

And then he grabbed the back of my head and held me to him and devoured my mouth, ravenous gulps that drew from every build of anticipation that had sparked between us.

I arched up against him and that movement dragged my clit along his cock again.

He consumed the moan I made, the noise echoing down his throat.

"Use me, Aphrodite," he said into me. "Bring yourself to orgasm on my cock."

"You aren't going to— *we* aren't going to—"

"Let them watch you ride you me." His words were caresses on my face as he trailed his lips to my ear. "Let them think we're fucking. That is all they will get. The sight of your face twisted in pleasure, the sounds you make. That alone is more than they deserve."

Relief had me moaning again, this time in fluttering, unhinged need. I was unable to get my lips to form anything beyond the action of kissing him. I couldn't stop, gravity mooring me to his body as I licked at the seam of his mouth and began to rock my hips.

His fingers clamped to me—one hand on my neck, one on the small of my back.

No demands came from the crowd. No cheers, no noise at

all. We could have been alone, if not for their eyes on us, the tension of their stunned confusion.

They had never seen a consummation like this.

I fell into a rhythm, rolling my hips back, thrusting up, the glide of his cock parting my wet lips so my swollen clit slid up and down his velvet hardness with each cadenced rock. I expected the ecstasy of this contact to plateau, but every movement only spurred me to want more, to *need* more, in a rising cyclone of fire and vitality.

Hephaestus pressed his nose to the side of my face, gasping, sweat beading on his forehead, dampening his neck where I held him. Every part of him was wound muscles, restraining his own release.

When my body began to shake, it broke a whimper out of me.

He gripped me tighter, using his hands to pulse my body in the rocking motion I had created. I couldn't continue, the sensation building, building, my thighs aching and my body going limp, but he guided me through it, and my whimper rose to a careening whine.

My head dipped back, face sheened, eyes fluttering shut. His lips delved onto my neck, sucking and biting the skin there, and that gentle pierce of his teeth sent a ricochet of pain straight to my clit.

I came, a manic, wailing scream of ecstasy, nerves alighting, colors spewing across my eyes in riots of gold and starlight. My cunt throbbed, reaching, clenching, and I felt my wetness thoroughly drenching his cock as I rode the tremors of orgasm on his iron erection.

He held me to him, cradling the back of my neck where my head was thrown to the ceiling. His gasps of breath were taut with pain, blasts of heated exhale into the bend of my shoulder.

We didn't speak, couldn't, locked in this high together, the falling down from it more like a gradual slip into silken warmth.

My lips found his again, and the kiss now was slow, unhurried.

But his cock was still hard between my legs.

He hadn't come.

What colossal restraint he had—what beautiful, remarkable control—

"You," I whimpered into his mouth. "You—"

"Do not worry for me," he pleaded, and I kissed my way across his face, to the rounded veins in his forehead, the sweat droplets gathered on his hairline. "What do you need? Are you all right?"

I panted, unable to catch my breath, licking at the salt of his skin, wanting to devour him whole. "I need you to come inside me," I told him. "I need you to fall apart between my legs."

He *roared*.

Hephaestus surged up from the bed, keeping my legs clasped around him, his hard cock lodged between us.

"The wedding is done," he shouted to the room, and he marched us through the crowd, kicking aside chairs; someone toppled to the floor with a cry, but he didn't stop, the heft of his iron boots banging with every step.

I looped my arms around his neck and sucked the lobe of his ear into my mouth as he carried me through the halls of Olympus. He half ran, half stumbled at times, cursing softly and groaning my name in such a pleading tear that I almost felt bad for tormenting him.

But now that I could taste him at will, I never wanted to stop.

Now that my body had felt even a fraction of what his could bring out in me, I would have to be renamed as the goddess of his pleasure only—there was no beauty in the world more exquisite than this.

14

Hephaestus

The halls passed, a blur.

She writhed against me, her wetness and warmth pressed directly over my cock, her teeth nibbling my ear and her voice pitching in a moan.

I ran. Slowed, turned a corner, bounded down halls, down, down into Olympus, cursing how far away my forge was from the bulk of this place. Never had I wanted to be close to the marbled halls; but now I envisioned rearranging the whole of this mountain just to accommodate the unabashed need that had taken thorough control.

This wasn't even need. It was a thing beyond. I had been unmade, no longer a god, not even a mortal, but something beneath, a hellish, crawling creature with one task and one task alone: to appease this goddess's command.

To come inside of her.

To fall apart between her legs.

At last, *at last*, I came upon my forge, kicked inside, and slammed the massive iron door behind us. I clamped her to me in one arm and used the other to throw the heavy bolt—rarely did I use it, but now, now, if anyone tried to interrupt us, it was for their own protection.

Her lips found mine again and for a moment I went still, tasting her mouth.

No one kissed in Olympus. All the orgies, all the fucking, and kisses were practically myth. Mouths were used for other things, not the intimacy in this contact between gasps and tongues and teeth. If the banquet hall had been struck by our consummation, her kissing me had been the final hammer of the final nail; they would know now, unabashedly, that she was mine, and I was hers, and we possessed a connection that Zeus himself could not sever.

I began walking again. I knew every corner of this forge, and so I steered us through the main room with my eyes shut, savoring the pulse of her soft, soft lips, the sweetness of her little tongue, the way I could get her breath to seize if I clamped my mouth over hers and demanded her full awareness.

I pushed us into a room—not my bedchamber.

The room I had prepared for her.

The flutter of the crystalline light catcher I had made sent sheens of blue over my closed lids, so when she gasped, I smiled, and leaned my forehead to her jaw, where she had twisted away to look.

"Hephaestus," she breathed. "It's beautiful."

"It's yours."

"Mine?"

I looked at her, zeal sinking into a sort of need that I had never felt before. All of this was something I had never felt before; to hold her and feel my stiff desire but embrace a slow pace, no desperate grasping, no frantic hands—it was sensual, it was appreciative. It was utterly worthy of *her*.

"I made this room for you," I told her. "For when—if—you would stay here with me."

Aphrodite turned back to face me, using her arms around my neck to press closer. "With you."

"Hm."

"Lay me down, Hephaestus."

She had been obedient in the banquet hall, and it was my turn now. I knelt and sat her on the edge of the mattress.

The angle put me in line with her cunt, and I found myself fighting to stay staring at her eyes—

But she lifted her skirt, peeling back that gold fabric, to show me how she had her legs spread wide.

Her cunt was as perfect as the rest of her. It shamed me to silence, sending a flare of simmering heat over me.

"You did this to me," she whispered, a pinched, throaty whine. "You brought my body to this."

She ran her fingers through her folds, showing the sheen, the tuft of dark hair matted in her wetness. She was a mess; I knew my cock was similarly drenched from her.

I could take no more. It had been only moments since I had sat her down, but it was too long to go without touching her.

I dove forward, scooping her ass into my arms, and angled her cunt for my mouth.

I feasted on her, my tongue laving up her thighs—those thighs, those thighs that made me want to be a poet—and I drove my face into the searing heat at her core. I opened my mouth to cover these lips as I had her others, slamming into her with insistent draughts as though nursing every last dreg from a goblet of wine.

"Hephaestus—" She threw back across the mattress, hands gripping the bedding. *"Hephaestus—"*

I directed my sucking and feasting to her clit, pulling the whole of that tender bud into my mouth.

Aphrodite bucked, her heels slamming against my back, digging into my spine. "Inside of me—need you inside of me—"

I needed her to come more.

I needed her to scream, for that noise to be the first part of her imprinted on my home's walls.

I suckled hard, nursing her clit with my tongue. She reared and writhed and begged, but I held strong, keeping her ass firmly in my arms, her body forced to my attentions.

When she came, I felt the nerves in her clit pulse and squirm just as frantically as her body, her piercing shriek of pleasure making drop after drop of precum surge from my cock.

"Please, please," she gasped, bleary, her fingers scrambling from the bedding to my head, to my shoulders, pulling at me. "Please, Hephaestus—"

I rose up her, surging my mouth to hers. "Do you taste yourself on me?"

She moaned into my lips.

I pulled at the buckle on the front of her strophion; it popped open and fell away. "Yours is the only cunt I will ever again devour." I tugged at her gown and she lifted up, arms limp, but did her best to help me undress her. "Your lips, the only ones I will ever again taste." She was naked in this bed I had made for her, in my home, this goddess was *naked for me*, and I was undone. "Your body is the only sheath my cock will ever again know."

"Yes," she whined, delirious in orgasm, "yes, Hephaestus, yes—"

Her breasts hung free, and I almost wept at their beauty—heavy and round, her nipples hardened and pink.

I dragged my hands up the soft rolls of her belly and wrapped my fingers around one breast. My cock strained, bucking, and I whimpered at the feel of her warm skin in my palm, that soft density, as I bent down and flicked her pointed nipple with the sharp tip of my tongue.

She cried out, body shaking with stimulation, and she leaned up onto one elbow to slide the fingers of her hand into my hair. Her fist clenched, as if bracing herself, but there would be no preparation for this, no way to stifle the onslaught.

I aligned my cock with her entrance.

Her breathing shallowed. Her blissed eyes widened to lock with mine, and there I held as I pushed inside of her.

I watched every muscle on her face. Every twitch, every pulse of her eyebrows, every flare of her pupils.

I had not gone more than a knuckle's depth when she sucked in a breath.

"Don't stop," she said, though, and I withdrew, just a little, to work the tip back in.

The *heat.* The tightness. The snug, crushing grip of her around me. I wanted to root to the hilt, fought to keep my hips from jutting forward. The smallness of her cunt made my cock look even more enormous; how would it fit? But it would, it would—

I stroked my thumb in smooth circles around her clit and she ground against my hand, pulling more of my cock into her with each thrust for pleasure.

Increment by increment, more of me entered her. In a little, out, in a little.

She went limp, falling back on the bed, and I curved my body over hers, holding her to me. Her breasts pressed to my chest, those hard nipples brushing across my skin.

"Are you all right?" I managed. Every moment of the past few hours had been an exercise in control, but this, this was the finale.

Aphrodite looked up at me, her eyes black with desire, and widened her legs for me in response.

I pressed down on her clit and drove home.

She cried out, throaty and high, and as a blossom of regret began to sprout, she dug her fingernails into my back in sudden claws.

"Fuck me, Hephaestus," she begged, throat ripping over the demand. "*Fuck me.*"

My body slammed into her, thrusting manically, helpless not to obey. The slap of our naked bodies filled the silence of our mutual, tangled focus.

She was beautiful. No—beautiful was not a strong enough word, not full enough for the complexity of her. I had never in my existence believed more in our manifestation from concepts: she was the embodiment of beauty. Her hair splayed across the bed, skin glistening with sweat, eyes locked on mine, red lips parted in coupled shock and ecstasy. She was unraveling and she was pleasure-limp and she was the pinnacle of anything that had ever come from this mountain.

Her gaze dropped between us and I reared back so she could see where we were joined, so *I* could see, watching in fogged amazement the proof of our coupling.

My cock was inside her, spreading her plump lips wide, the moisture of her smearing white on me with each pull out and thrust back in.

She had let me not only touch her, but enter her, be the first—be the only, if she would give it—and I could not convince myself that this was not some sort of cruel dream.

She reached for me, dragging me back to lay atop her, and I hefted my arms under her knees to position her and—*there*. That spot, my cock driving in, that was the one she needed.

"Hephaestus," she sobbed, my name breaking apart on my rocking thrusts.

Never had a goddess been more worthy of the title.

Never had a face looked a more perfect blend of trance and grounding.

I angled deeper, and she wailed, her cunt seizing around my cock with a mind-shattering tightness.

"I'm going to come in you," I gasped, a warning, a beg for her permission. "I'm going to come apart in this cunt, Goddess."

"Yes, yes, *Hephaestus*," she screamed, her body quivering, and I exploded in her, hot jetting streams as my hips gave one final thrust, a roughened snarl tearing out of my throat until it became her name, just her name, over and over.

"Aphrodite, Aphrodite," I prayed, face buried in her neck, worshipping, worshipping, and I would continue to worship, for as long as she let me, her most fervent acolyte, her truest priest.

15

Aphrodite

I came to consciousness in such bliss that I feared I may have passed beyond Olympus. What time I had spent in this mountain had been strung with unease, so this feeling of contented harmony? I had ascended. It was the only explanation.

I twisted onto my back, blankets tangling around my body, and stretched, feeling that languid joy relaxing every muscle. The room came together around me, heavy, dark walls set to shimmers by the light catcher Hephaestus had made—azure and diamond white and deepest teal.

My hands spread across the bed, searching.

It was empty.

I bolted upright, holding the blankets to my chest.

Concern began to rise, but before I could even call out, the door opened.

He slipped inside, balancing a tray in one hand, a pitcher of water in the other.

He saw me awake and stopped.

Just the touch of his eyes, and every caress from last night flashed through me, burning my cheeks to crimson and making me pull my legs to my chest, unable to contain the flurry of memory. He, too, flushed, his eyes tempering, and he tipped his head as a smile crawled across his face.

"Good morning," he said.

I was caught in the way his full lips moved around the words. Those lips that had been affixed to my clit, to my nipple, to my neck, to every erotic part of my body.

"Good morning," I managed, and I knew I sounded needy still. I didn't care.

I was the Goddess of Love, and I knew it now in droves—the way love could be an act, physical and poetic, bodies dancing in an unspoken choreograph. Some part of me had come alive; my creation only days ago had been incomplete until last night. I understood the fullness of my purpose now, the breadth of what could be tapped from this facet of love, and I felt a sort of craze sparking giddy and wild in my chest, to grab his wrist and pull him back and explore these new discoveries until I dissolved back into the sea froth I had come from.

A pleated kilt hung around his hips, but he looked as disheveled as I felt, his hair mussed. There was a smear of my lipstick on his neck, a print of my mouth on his chest.

And when he turned to shut the door, I saw the lingering scratches my nails had torn into his back.

"I hurt you!" How had his god-might not healed those wounds already?

Hephaestus set his offering at the foot of the bed and hovered over the tray. It was spread with food, an almost laughable amount. "I was not sure what you liked." He sorted through fruit, pastries, cheeses. "Nor what you might have even had time to sample yet. I may have gone overboard—"

"Hephaestus. Your *back*."

He peeked up at me. And grinned. "I know."

"It hasn't healed."

"I know."

"But *how*?" I crawled closer to him, letting the blanket fall away, and even though we had had each other four times last night—five, one final time where he had licked me in a fog of collapsing pleasure—the moment his gaze bounced to my body, I sizzled with desire.

"How?" he echoed. His grinning eyes slid up to mine. "I have chosen not to let it heal, Goddess. I wore it as a mark of you as I retrieved us food. All of Olympus saw—or at least servants, and they will gossip. Now." He motioned to the tray. "What would you like?"

I had marked him, as I had dreamed of him marking me, and he let those scratches linger, treated them as a hard-earned trophy.

My teeth bore down into my lip.

His grin turned sly at my expression. "You need to eat first."

"Hardly."

"Aphrodite—"

"We are immortal."

"That does not mean you do not benefit from nourishment!" He handed me a cup of water.

I took it, drank, and tossed the empty cup into the bedding. "There. Now, you are wearing far too many clothes."

His cheeks pinked. He shook his head to the tray and sucked his teeth and looked at me with exasperation and weakening resolve.

But something else pulsed in his eyes. A wavering belief I had seen too often last night—disbelief that this was real.

Unworthiness to be here. Fear that it would vanish.

I could not bear that any part of him felt that I would leave him.

I reached out and cupped his face, stroking my thumb through his short beard. "How can I gain your trust?"

That made him jerk back to his full height. "What?"

"You do not trust that I want to be here."

He sat on the bed, gathering my hands into his and pulling them to his mouth, breathing me in.

"It is not you," he said finally. He looked up at me, his eyes glassy. "Joy is fragile in Olympus. I had something similar, once—something far, far less than *you*, than what you have given me, and losing that almost destroyed me. So to know how much you have come to mean to me, and to know also how very skilled this mountain is in snuffing out happiness? I do not trust the walls we live in, Aphrodite. I do not trust the forces around us. But you?" He held my hands to his chest and drew a breath I felt rattle against my palms. "If you say you are happy with me, that this morning has not brought you a surge of regret, then that is the future to which I will commit myself utterly. Your happiness is my only purpose now."

I pushed into his arms and kissed him.

Each time I had initiated kisses last night, it had seemed to shock him, until he had started kissing me back in innocent wonder. And now, he scooped me to him, crushing my lips to his, and I had to fight to pull back enough to say into him, "I am happy. I am happier than I believed to be possible here. You have quickly become my only purpose, too, and I—"

But my own words made me jolt back with a gasp.

Hephaestus tensed immediately, but I didn't wait for him to ask.

"The war!" I gripped his massive shoulders. "Helen and Paris. I forgot to check on them!"

Hephaestus rolled his eyes shut with a curse. "I promised I would bring you to the orb room after the wedding. I failed you, Goddess. I should have checked on my own mortals as well."

I leaned forward, my breasts pressing to his chest, and I felt the heat that contact stoked in him. "Do not take all the blame. I was distracting you, if memory serves." I straightened. "But I would like to check on them."

"Of course." Hephaestus moved to the trunk against the wall. He drew out my gown from last night—when had he laid it in there with such thought? He draped it against the bed and frowned. "You will wish to return to your suite as well."

He said it without looking at me.

I did, at least, want to speak to my nymphs, to tell them what had happened.

Did he mean I would stay in my suite? That I would not return to his home? Did I *want* to live here, with him, or did I want to keep my own space?

I had no particular claim on the rooms I had been given. But him? I wanted to be wherever he was.

"Yes," I said slowly. I licked my lips in thought. "How . . . how does it work in Olympus? With gods who are married. Do you wish me to stay in my suite? Will you call on me when . . . when you have need of me?"

I did not realize until I asked it how little I wanted that.

I did not want to be in those rooms, pacing, waiting ever on his need. My own need did not seem capable of waning; I would go mad with counting the moments until I was back with him—

Hephaestus dropped to his knees beside me. "Goddess. What do you want?"

I want you to want me as passionately as I have come to want you.

I am terrified—

"Aphrodite." He put his hand on the side of my face. "Tell me what you are thinking. Now."

His tone was so demanding that my lips parted, and I heard my own voice come out fast and grating, panicked at having been caught in something.

"I want you to ask me to stay here with you," I admitted.

His brows went slack, but he continued to study me intently. "And?"

"And?"

"Why does that make you afraid?"

"I do not understand how this works still," I said, and I felt tears burn my eyes. "You have promised me so much, and I do not know if that was in the throes of sex or if it is something I can fall on. More, I do not know how I will even begin to earn those promises from you—who am I? A new goddess? And you are—you are—"

I scrambled for words to describe him. But everything fell short, and so I closed my eyes and tears dripped down my cheeks and Hephaestus pulled my forehead to his, our breaths mingling in the silence of my stifled sobs.

"I have rushed you into so much, Goddess," he whispered. "Forgive me. I forget, as all here have, that you are so new to us. I will slow down—"

"I do not want you to slow down."

"But you need it."

"I need you." My fingers dragged through the hairs on his

chest. "I can endure all the trials of Olympus if I have you at my side. That is what I need."

He kissed me, a quick, sweet stroke of his lips. "You have me. You have me for as long as you desire."

"That." I pulled back and looked at him through my tears. "That is what unsettles me. You give me the sole power in this relationship—and while I know you do so to give me agency, and I appreciate you for it, it terrifies me that you might one day think I have abandoned you, when in reality it is Ares taking advantage or a norm of Olympus I did not understand. I need to know that I have you, that you will come for me, no matter what you might believe I want. I am telling you now, Hephaestus—I am yours, and I demand you fight to keep what is yours. Forever."

He rocked, dropping forward to press his fists to the bedding. "Aphrodite."

"Swear it."

"You are mine." His words grew rougher as he looked up at me, eyelids heavy. "You are mine, and I will fight to keep what is mine."

"Forever."

"Forever."

I wiped my cheeks, breathing once into the cup of my hands, before I nodded decisively. "Take me to the orb room now."

But he did not rise to his feet.

"Do you understand," he started, the coarseness of his voice turning to almost a snarl, "how much restraint you are asking of me, after a speech like that, for me to take you to the orb room and not mount you against the wall right now?"

The vision speared deep into my gut. He had not taken me anywhere but in the bed yet, and I flicked my eyes to the wall, letting the image sink in, a delicious shiver.

"I will be quick at the orb," I said.

"Yes," he told me. A command.

He helped me dress, affixed the strophion to me, and though I knew I was still a mess—the state of my hair, my smeared make up, wrinkles in my gown—I did not care. Nothing else mattered outside of checking on the war, and then returning to the cocoon of Hephaestus's home.

He had said he had had something similar to us in the past. Had he been married before? I would have to ask him. I could not imagine anyone here being worthy of him, the flighty, frivolous gods and nymphs too hollow for serious, selfless Hephaestus. But I wanted to know who had captured his heart. I wanted to know all the facets of his soul with as much thoroughness as I was coming to learn all the facets of his body.

Hephaestus pushed open the orb room and I let my gaze linger over the door again, admiring ever his skill in creating each mortal. He smiled at my fascination—it was rare for anyone to appreciate him.

It would be rare no longer.

The orb glowed its warm blue still, and I approached, nerves suddenly dampening my palms.

I had only wanted to bless those mortals, who had seemed to find each other so easily. How could a gift from a goddess have caused a war? Surely it was not so severe. Surely I would look and see it resolved.

Hephaestus stood next to me. He gave a firm nod and extended his own palm.

Hand shaking, I touched the orb, and he followed suit.

My mind filled with images, that now familiar clash of sights and people. I narrowed my focus—Paris and Helen. Troy. The war.

A rush and pull, and before me, I saw a massacre.

Bodies spread across a barren field, spears impaling them to the dirt. Arrows riddled carcasses. Flies buzzed around rotting heaps of flesh and refuse turned rancid under a high, bright sun. Wails echoed, the lament of families searching for loved ones; and beyond, war encampments, one against the walls of a massive city, the other on a glittering beach.

As if overlaid, a dream atop a vision, I saw other gods in that battlefield. Ares, blood-streaked and smug, reclining amid the bodies—he had the stench of victory about him. Apollo was there now too, glowing in gold armor. Athena, a more refined version of Ares; and others—they all moved about the carnage as though they did not see it, as though it did not affect them.

The vision shifted, and I saw within that city, in a palace at its center, Paris and Helen. Helen stood at a window, staring out at the field of battle, tears streaming down her face. Paris held her, turned her to him, kissed her, stroked her hair. But his face was gaunt; he was terrified.

What had they done?

What had *I* done?

I ripped my hand off the orb and stumbled back, muscles weakening so I collapsed on the floor, unable to breathe.

"Aphrodite!" Hephaestus was there immediately, so reminiscent of Paris's sweet comfort, and I grasped him, crawling up into his arms, though what right did I have to seek comfort when so many mortal lives had been lost because of my actions?

I pushed back, eyes blurring with tears, but I could not get my fingers to let go of Hephaestus's arms.

He tried to pull me back into the cage of him, but I shook

my head.

"Aphrodite," he said, "let me hold you."

Again, I shook my head. "Did you see it too?"

He nodded. "I looked in on the mortals I know are there. The ones I have blessed."

"Are all wars like that? Bodies. Blood. Death and rot—"

"Yes. Sometimes worse. They are never poetic, although mortal poets try to capture it as such. It is only ever grotesque."

"How did love cause that?" I gasped. "How can love be so destructive?"

"Love was not the cause, Aphrodite." Hephaestus stroked my hair behind my ear. "Love is what will make the war end. Love is what will make the war worthwhile. My mortals there—that is why I blessed them, with the skill and craftsmanship and vision I can, because I know things like that will enable them to endure."

My body went still.

I stood, and he followed me up, but I was in a scramble.

He was right. Love would be the force to pull them out of this war.

So love, I would give them.

I put my hand back on the orb. Paris and Helen were in my vision again, now seated next to each other on a bed.

As I had once before, I heaped my blessing on them. That their love would endure above all. That it would be preserved, even if war threatened to rip it apart.

Other mortals came to me throughout Troy, and in the Greek encampment too. Some solitary, some together; I dotted similar blessings throughout this war. Love, beauty, small anchors that would infuse everyone in the war's darkest moments.

I lifted my hand from the orb, tears drying on my face.

"How will I know it is enough?" I whispered.

Hephaestus ran his hands up and down my arms. "That is up to them. We can only do as much as we are able."

"Which is how much? How often do you come?"

"Every few days, more frequently if I am able. Time moves differently for mortals, though; a day here could be many for them."

I leaned back into him, a chill creeping into my body. "Take me home, Hephaestus."

He encircled my waist with his arms and pressed his face into my hair, a low, throaty rumble reverberating in him. "I like the way you say that. My home is yours now."

"Yes."

"Say it." He sunk his teeth lightly into my neck.

I hissed and arched back against him, and under his tender workings, the remnants of stress faded. "Your home is mine. Your bed is mine. This body—" I moved his hand from my waist to my cunt. "—is yours."

His breath came out hard and hot against the side of my neck. "We have one more stop."

My suite. My nymphs would be concerned—and I did want to explain all that had happened.

That jostled another thought loose. "Could you make more strophions? First for my nymphs."

Hephaestus's arms tightened around me. He kissed up the side of my face. "Of course."

"Can I help you?"

His lips unfurled in a smile I felt press to my cheek. "You want to learn metalworking, Goddess?"

"I do."

"Anything for you. Anything."

He meant it. The weight in his words had a gravity that hooked in the core of me, tugging gently.

But I felt an echo of foreboding.

We were married; his claim on me was complete; I had this strophion even to protect me, and I would begin to ensure that my nymphs and any others in Olympus were safe the same way.

But why did it feel as though we were all too similar to Helen and Paris, standing on the edge of something grim that would seek to rip apart our love?

How could the strongest power I possessed feel so fragile?

16

Hephaestus

Mortals were the ones whose lives pivoted irrevocably on lightning-fast moments. A sword ending a life, a child being born, lovers finding each other—gods had long envied humans for those moments most of all, the jarring heave of change that could upend an otherwise dreary existence.

But in the span of one night, she had irreversibly changed me as though I was a life-soft mortal.

I understood her fear. So new to Olympus, and already she recognized how much of a threat something like this was to the other gods. They had been envious of me for fucking her as it was—but once they saw the way we were truly enraptured by each other? As soon as my siblings recognized the presence of something *new*—love, true and pure—they would set upon it like vultures.

So as we walked through the marbled halls of Olympus, I was careful to keep from touching her. She eyed me questioningly but accepted it, though she kept her body close to mine, especially as we passed the open-doored rooms where other gods lay, feasting or listening to music or fucking.

Some called out to us, asking for details of the wedding night—*"I heard of the scratches she gave you, Hephaestus! Proof she didn't want you, eh?"*

The fools.

But let them think that that was the cause of my marks; the longer they believed that she was with me against her will, the better.

I kept walking, firmly steering her with my hand on the small of her back, until we finally, *finally*, reached her suite.

I routed the halls between her room and my forge, playing over and over the fastest path. We would speak to her nymphs, get her things, and return to the safety of my home—our home—as fast as possible.

Aphrodite pushed inside.

A flurry of three squealing bodies descended on her.

"You're *back!*"

"Wearing the same *gown*—Goddess!"

"How are you? Sit down!" the last voice was kindest, and I softened to her as she led Aphrodite to a chair by a window that showed the sea.

The nymphs barely looked at me. If they did, it was cursory half-glances they hid with shudders and quick turns of their back.

They feared me. As they feared Ares? Or because of my iron boots, because of my reputation?

Either way, I lingered by the closed door, arms folded, and watched the nymphs flutter about my wife.

My wife.

I couldn't help my grin.

Aphrodite took the hand of a nymph who tucked her hair

back, grabbed a damp towel to wipe her day-old makeup. "I'm fine, Thalia, truly. It was a lovely ceremony."

"Lovely?" Thalia knelt at Aphrodite's feet as she worked. "I heard . . ." Her eyes cast to me. "I heard he did not even undress you. That he made you ride him. That he—"

She touched Thalia's cheek. "It was what I wanted. Thalia, I am happy."

The nymph didn't seem to understand the word. And I realized, with a sinking weight in my chest, that she wouldn't. Few in Olympus understood it.

"I am moving to Hephaestus's forge," Aphrodite said. "I need some of my things—"

One of the nymphs chirped protest. Another swatted that one's arm. "Aglaea! Calm!"

"But—the *forge*, my lady?" Aglaea's face had gone pale. "In the dark deep of the mountain?"

"Yes."

"But—I—"

"You may stay on in my suite here," Aphrodite said. "I do not imagine it will need to be given to another god? So you are welcome to stay, and if any ask, simply tell them that I am currently away but will be returning soon. Then, if I am truly needed, you know to find me at the forge."

The three nymphs stared at her in unbridled shock.

I did, too.

She was giving this suite—a suite fit for a *goddess*—to three nymphs?

No other god would have thought to do such a thing. They would have cast off their servants without a second thought, or dragged them along to the forge. But, clearly, Aphrodite felt the same desire for privacy that I did—she looked up at me with a small smile.

I beamed back at her.

My wife.

My amazing, generous, caring wife.

Thalia was weeping. "Goddess—you do too much for us."

"I will do more—Hephaestus and I will begin work on your strophions."

"Goddess!"

"Thank you, Thalia." Aphrodite leaned forward, cradling the nymph's face in her hands. "I do not think I would have gotten through the first moments of my creation without you."

Thalia nodded but couldn't speak, and as Aphrodite turned to the others, giving them the same focused thanks, Thalia stood and faced me.

"Thank you, God," she said and gave a deep curtsy.

I shook my head. "It is unnecessary."

"I assure you," she peeked up at me, her eyes red with tears, set with a fear that was slowly, painfully, beginning to lift, "it means everything."

I had berated myself for how long it had taken me to think of making enchanted protection for Aphrodite.

Now, that self-flagellation returned tenfold.

I had spent the past decades since my greatest failure bemoaning all I had not been able to do in the face of Olympus's greed and lust. I knew what fate awaited those who resisted the advances of stronger gods. And yet, I had sulked in my failure, which had only reinforced that failure, hadn't it? I had never tried to *do* anything to keep what had happened before from happening again.

"Three strophions for you," I said to Thalia. "But do you know of others who would want one?"

Her eyebrows rose. "The servants said Apollo was blasted across the room. They said it took him a full day to recover."

"And so?"

"And so I know dozens who would want such a thing," she whispered, reverent.

My burning sense of remorse tangled up with a rising tide of focus, the set and purpose of a task I had, a mission. My mind spun with preparations and I nodded at Thalia.

"It will be done. If I get them to you, can you distribute them? Secrecy is best used."

It would not be difficult for the gods to find out where such protective items had come from—I could not make them all strophions. Rings and necklaces and bracelets too, maybe, varied things so they would be less obvious.

Thalia nodded. "Of course, my lord. Of course!"

Aphrodite came up alongside Thalia. Sometime in the conversation, her other nymphs had coaxed her into a fresh gown—sky-blue and simple, showing her cleavage in a too-tempting slit. The strophion was reaffixed over it.

"What are you two planning?" she asked.

"Your new husband is too kind," Thalia said, her throat catching.

"My husband." Aphrodite rolled the words across her tongue. The grin she gave yanked my cock to half-hardness—that we had not realized the titles we now had for each other until this moment had every thought in my mind funneling fast towards getting her back to my forge.

Thalia bowed to me, to Aphrodite. "I will pack your things, Goddess, and see them delivered to the forge in secret. None will know that you do not live here anymore."

"Thank you, Thalia." Aphrodite bent forward and hugged

the nymph.

She melted against Aphrodite. Then went rigid. "Goddess! I—" She glanced up at me, then twisted to whisper quietly to my wife. I heard, though, as she said, "What should I do with the necklace Ares gave you?"

He had given her a necklace? I frowned—

But Aphrodite shook her head. "Whatever you like. It is of no matter to me."

She turned with a smile and took my hand.

"Now," she said, her eyes focused again fully on mine, and my heart centered. "Take me home."

I carried a basket of a few items for her, extra clothing she could use immediately, some makeups and soaps and sweet-smelling perfumes that clashed with the dark masculinity of my forge. But it was a clash that I welcomed as I set the basket down in the room I had made for her.

I did not think I would be returning to my own bedroom any time soon.

Aphrodite knelt by the basket and began removing items, laying gowns out across the bed.

"Can I help?" I started to bend next to her, but she waved me away.

"It will not take long. Can we start on the strophions after I have finished?"

I smiled at her. That she wanted to learn my craft had me tugging uncomfortably at the tightness of my cock pushing against my leather kilt. "Are you certain that is what you wish to start on?"

My tone pulled her eyes up to me.

She flushed, her hands lowering to her lap, tangled up with

a strip of red silk. "I need to know they are safe, too," she said, but she worried her lip, her eyes going liquid as she surveyed my body, still shirtless, still marked by her lipstick. "I think this could truly help many in Olympus. There is beauty to be found here, and for too long it has been buried beneath force and presumption. This could, I think, allow others security to see that beauty."

I touched her cheek with my thumb. "That selflessness will only make my next taking of you all the sweeter. I will prepare a workspace."

Her lips curved into a grin and she twisted to kiss my palm. "My husband truly is too kind."

I moaned. My thumb pressed against her lips until she parted them, and I felt the feather-soft lick of her tongue as I pumped in.

"Ah, Aphrodite—" I hissed and ripped back from her with a forceful throat-clear. "I will be in my forge inventing the fastest way possible to make enchanted items. Your body is not merely my muse, but my motivation."

She beamed at me as I put my back to her and left the room, my hard cock wailing at me with every step. How long had it been since I had been inside her? Hours? Disgraceful that so much time had passed.

I pulled out my finer work tools, a low table set with my jewelry making supplies. Much of it was still arranged from when I had made her strophion, so I did not have a lot to do—but I picked up that jar of gold again. There was something off about it still. I had not used so much, had I? Why was it lighter? And the powder I used in my enchantments—was I truly running so low? I would have to commission more from Zeus.

But it scratched at me still. I hadn't used that much.

Where had it gone?

Unease gave way quickly to that waiting, stalking regret. I *should have* used it. I had at my fingers the solution to the problem that had made me a recluse, that haunted my dreams, and I had not thought to use it, not once. My only powers went into making enchanted weapons, immobilizing nets and strength-enhancing swords, things my siblings used to slaughter mortals.

But to make protective items for the nymphs and gods and demigods who were victimized by Olympus?

I was such a fool.

Aphrodite had changed that.

I set out my molds and picked a variety of designs—a few strophions, but necklaces too, thick bands that wouldn't easily snap; rings; cuff bracelets. Some would be enchanted with lightning, but that would be quickly noted as well—better to have variety in everything. So others would enact violent illness. Some would cause searing internal pain.

Honestly, imagining the ways I would make my siblings suffer gave me far too much joy.

It truly was an embarrassment that I had not thought of this sooner.

Awhile later, I felt gentle fingers on my shoulders. "You get tense here when you work."

That muscle relaxed under her thumbs, prying circles into my skin. "Hazard of the job," I said, half focused on fitting together a mold for a cuff. I glanced up at her. "Are you ready to begin?"

She nodded and reached past me to pick up a small mold, one for a ring. "Not a strophion?"

I told her my plan. The varied items, the effects. She listened raptly, eyes darting through mine, equal parts awe and interest.

"This is more than I could have hoped for," she breathed when I was done. "They will love it. Thank you."

I turned back to the bench, her gratitude rubbing raw the spot inside of me that was already bloodied from regret. "I do not deserve thanks. This is years late."

"Years?" She sat on a stool next to me, her legs opened towards me.

I flattened my hands on the worktable.

This goddess had come to see parts of me that no one else on Olympus knew. She had awoken parts of me that I myself had not known.

And yet she still did not know the greatest scar in me, and she had not even asked, had not even glanced at my iron boots in all the times last night when I had not taken them off.

It was because of that, partially, that I was able to prop my elbows on the table and look out into my forge and breathe, the iron-damp air rolling into my lungs.

"Her name was Cabeiro," I said.

Aphrodite shifted closer. Her hand settled on my lap.

"She was a demigod." I picked up a mold and a knife and worked at a chunk of gold that had been stuck in it last time I had formed a ring. "I'd wanted to marry her. I had thought she wanted the same. When I asked her—she'd recoiled. We had fucked already, but in secret, and I realized she was ashamed of what we had done. She said she could not be known to be the *Soot God's Whore*."

"Hephaestus," my name burst out and her fingers tensed on my leather kilt.

I shook my head. "That was not unexpected." It had not

been the first someone had said something like that to me; but it had been the deepest. "What came next, though." I pried at the gold stuck in the mold. Pried, and pried, the knife bending in my grip. "She joined an orgy. I watched—I attended them back them. I didn't participate, but I was there, and she watched me the whole while that she serviced others, and I thought—perhaps she is teasing me? This is a game. And then the orgy . . . turned. As you have seen they do."

Aphrodite's whole body tensed.

"Somehow, Ares found out I had proposed to Cabeiro," I said. "She told him, I think. He declared that the first to catch her would claim her."

I forced myself to look at her. To see the stain of red on her cheeks, the horror in her eyes.

"Cabeiro ran, laughing, at first. But Ares was all bloodshed back then. Apollo, and Athena, and Dionysus—they fed into his insanity. Chased Cabeiro all the way to Ares's rooms, high in Olympus, second only to Zeus's. She ran, and I followed, and she stopped laughing when they caught her, and I tried—I *tried*—but there is a window in Ares's room." My hands shook too much. I dropped my tools and spread my fingers as if sizing that window, but it was pointless to try to hide these emotions. "We fell."

My voice broke.

I was staring into my forge, but I saw that fall, the whipping sea wind, the moisture of the clouds, the rushing tear of Cabeiro's scream and the sudden, jarring snap of impact.

"A fall like that. From the very top of Olympus." I swallowed. "For even a god, it was devastating." I waved at my iron boots. "But she was only a demigod. She didn't survive."

Aphrodite cupped the back of my neck. She didn't speak,

and I leaned closer to her, her silence insistent, warm.

"I woke up here." I breathed through the ache. "I couldn't walk. My feet—even all the god-might in my body can't heal them. It was only after I managed to make these braces and hobble out of my forge that I found out what had happened."

"Wait." Aphrodite put her other hand on my shoulder. "The gods left you here? Alone?"

I nodded.

There was a new weight in her silence. It drew my eyes to her, and I saw, for the first time, what rage looked like on her face.

It was not beautiful.

It was petrifying.

"They left you alone," she repeated. Her fingers tightened on my arm, my neck. "I want to destroy them. To make them suffer for having hurt you."

"Now you know how I feel when they touch you."

"And why you are so driven by this project." She unclamped her fingers from my neck and brushed them across my cheekbone. "You are fixing what happened then. Righting the wrong."

"Too late."

"Not for those you help," she told me. "Not for Thalia, for Aglaea, for Euphrosyne. Not for the others who you will save."

"Not for you." I pressed her hand to my face. "I promised myself I would not let it happen to you, either. And I will keep that promise, Goddess."

She smiled, such unfiltered adoration in her eyes that I felt the last vestiges of my restraint loosen, and tears slipped free.

"I know, Hephaestus," she whispered, catching my tears with her thumb. "I know."

17

Aphrodite

Hephaestus gave me an apron—one of his, and so it was massive on my smaller frame, but I knotted the band around twice and shortened the neck loop and it was passable.

Then we bent over his worktable, and he showed me his universe.

Jewelry crafting was finer work, he explained; someday, he would teach me how to use the full of the forge, how to hammer and shape and fill the air with sparks. But for now, we worked with small bursts of heat, tinges of orange-hot pokers that melted gold and commanded silver to obey. Even so, the work was sweaty, violent heat that had us quickly drenched.

But I couldn't get enough. Not of his instruction, patient and kind. Not of watching him work, the flex of his muscles attuned to this, the fervor in his eyes when a project completed and it fit his high standards.

It was the same fervor he had shown over my body last night.

We worked, and feasted on the food he had brought earlier, and somewhere in the middle of waiting for a layer of metal to cool on a strophion, I couldn't take the heat any longer.

He had a barrel of water in the corner, fed by a tube from within the mountain, and the water within was blissfully cool and crisp.

I dipped a bucket in and dumped the whole of it over my head.

"Aphrodite!" he exclaimed with a bellowing laugh. "I have a bath here, you know."

"I do not know, actually." I wiped the water from my eyes, hair hanging in a matted sheet around me. I grinned at him. "I have seen the bedroom and your forge. Nothing more. Not that there need be more."

He began to crack open a mold, split between a timer counting down in his head and the water dripping from my body. "That room—there. Undress. I will join you."

"Will you?"

His thick hands worked the mold. "Ah—yes, are you joking? Yes. That will never be a lie."

"Hm." My gaze cast around the forge.

He had allowed me into his space. The work of it, this sanctuary for him, but also the story he had shared.

Soot God's Whore.

It was good that Cabeiro was not here. She would feel the full brunt of my hatred for her, to call him such a thing. Already I did not know how I would face the other gods, knowing how they had treated him. To leave him, hurt and maimed, *alone*—to mock him for his injury, to sneer at him—

I had felt the thrill of promises made from him, and so I knew if I promised him similar things, they would resonate. But how could I show him that the other gods were wrong to treat him as they had, that he was so far above them, and that I was so stunningly proud to be his?

He was twisted towards the table, his back to me as I worked my gown off but left the apron on. I had removed my strophion the moment we had returned to the forge, and the sheer fabric of my dress was destroyed, sweat-stained and the hem splattered with dirt. My body beneath was worse, I knew, but it stoked honor suddenly. I had at last been marked by him, in a way, by the force of his work.

The mold broke free and he hummed his approval of the strophion as it clattered to the table. "Good. There—"

He turned.

I strode to the forge, showing myself in profile, nude beneath his leather apron. The coals within were not stoked to their full heat, but still they simmered, and when I approached, more sweat broke across my spine, beading down my shoulder blades.

"Goddess," he said. "What are you doing? Do you not want a bath?"

"Only if you cannot handle me like this," I said over my shoulder. "But I think you can."

I bent back against the side of the forge. The heat scalded my skin, not to burning, only on the bare end of discomfort.

"You promised to mount me against a wall." My voice was slipping lower, breathy. I was not good yet at speaking sultry, the way he could; I was too easily consumed in my desire. "Do not break your promise to me, husband."

I watched him swallow. The glow of the enchanted lights in the ceiling, white and bright, danced with the heave of the forge, orange and gold, and those colors met on his face, bejeweled his surprise.

"There is a wall in the bath," he managed, eyes fixed to the edge where the apron cut across the side of my breast.

I arched, chest pushing out. "This is your haven," I said, a question.

He nodded.

"Then make it mine as well."

Hephaestus teetered forward, drawn in slow steps by the force of my eyes on him. "I am filthy," he said, halfway to me, holding out his black-streaked hands in a helpless show.

"Yes," I said. "And I want all of it. All the parts of you, Hephaestus. All your filth, all your passion, all your scars."

He reached me, and the light in his eyes was a smoldering flame that flared as he scooped my head in his hand and plunged his tongue into my mouth. I fell open for him, hands splayed on the burning wall of the forge, letting him kiss me, letting him feel the sweat on my face and the dampness of my hair.

"I do not deserve you," he moaned into me.

"You do," I promised, begged. "Prove how much you do."

He ground his forehead to mine with a deep-throated snarl. "You do not know what you ask."

"Show me." I knotted my fingers in the strap of his apron, holding him close to me. "I have much to learn, don't I? Teach me, Hephaestus. I need you," I undid the tie at my apron's neck strap and let it fall, revealing my bare breasts, glistening in the light, streaked with soot, "to show me."

He grabbed one immediately and dropped his mouth to mine, kissing me deep and long as he massaged my breast. He had learned quickly how to yank incoherent whines from me, and he did so now: taking my nipple between his knuckle and thumb, squeezing so gently, rolling so slightly. I mewled, going nearly limp, and he peeled back with a sultry grin.

"Wait here," he said and slipped off into his forge.

He was gone only a moment, hardly long enough for me to catch my breath, and when he reappeared he touched my chin.

"You ask to learn," he whispered into my mouth. "Then let me teach you how much pleasure can be drawn from this body, Goddess."

I nodded, already unable to speak. This god dragged me into delirium at a rapid-fire pace.

"If it is too much," he continued, dragging his nose across my cheek, "say the word *iron*. Then I will know you are at your limit—but otherwise, beg me, plea, fall apart. You want to see every part of me? I would have every part of you. Show me what you look like at your most unraveled."

"Yes," I hissed.

He hesitated, face pressed to the side of mine, and I felt the hitch in his breath. "When we met, I said if you had been a thing, I would have locked you away in my forge."

"I—I remember."

"Allow me to do that. To display you as the sole focal point of beauty in this heated forge of dirt and metal."

He showed me one of the objects he had retrieved. A set of manacles.

I made a noise like a cry, only stifled, in the far of my throat.

I had wanted to see what he could do with my body.

Now, I would know.

I held out my wrists.

He took both of them in one hand and lifted my arms. There was a hook on the ceiling I hadn't noticed, one of dozens for his projects—he threaded the manacles through, and attached them to me.

I hung before him, my feet still on the ground, but I couldn't

141

slow my breathing, breasts bare, the apron still covering the lower half of me.

Strung up like this, I was utterly at his mercy.

My clit throbbed, swollen already, and I threw my head back, eyes slamming shut.

"Look at me, Goddess," he demanded. "I want you to see what I do to you."

I obeyed, hazy, leaning my cheek against one of my sweaty arms.

My eyes locked on his hand, where he lifted something else. It looked similar to tools we had used to craft some of the enchanted items, only far smaller, with a twisted screw on one end that he cranked open.

He bent his head and licked at my nipple, hardening it, that razor edge of his tongue driving my body to thrashing on the manacles.

"Breathe, Goddess," he said, his voice hoarse as he pinched the thick part of my breast and attached the device. It was a clamp, and the moment he released it, it latched onto my nipple with a shock of pressure bordering on pain.

My body jolted like a lightning strike had plummeted from my head to my toes. A crooning whine echoed in my throat, but I bit it down, eyes shutting, every bit of focus going to my nipple, to the feeling there.

He moved to the other breast, attached another clamp, and I reeled, bucking, grateful for the manacles; I would be on my knees without them, thrashing on the floor in this wild mix of blinding pleasure and pain.

Hephaestus slid his hand under the apron and his fingers played between my legs. I was slick already, I knew; and when he pinched my clit, my eyes flew open.

I gaped at him. He couldn't—

He slid another clamp between my lips and expertly, skillfully, attached it to my clit.

I screamed. An orgasm tore through me, abrupt and forced and almost agonizing in its intensity, but unlike the others, there was no coming down—the stimulation remained, squeezing and squeezing, no rest, no pause. What I had come to learn as the end of pleasure now drew into new heights of ecstasy, my body wrenched into a fogged state of demanded, prolonged bliss.

Hephaestus lifted my legs into his hands, the apron pooling in my lap. Each shift tugged the clamps, my breasts, my clit, those three points so oversensitive that I could only hang there in mingled moans and screams.

"Tell me how you feel, Aphrodite," he said, and he sounded just as wrung out as I felt.

"I feel—" I swallowed, fighting for breath. "I can't—I can't, Hephaestus—"

It was too much, all of it—I couldn't come down, like waves crashing continuously, like a storm that wouldn't end.

"Can't what? Tell me. Speak to me." He shoved his cock deep into my pussy.

I wailed as my back slammed into the forge. The combination of that wall and the manacles let both of Hephaestus's hands roam free, and he cupped my breasts, the clamps shaking, flashing sparks of sensation in the very tips of my nipples.

"I can't—" I tried again. "I can't focus—the pleasure is everywhere, it doesn't end, it doesn't end, Hephaestus—"

"I can see the tension on your face." He thrust into me, and the clamp on my clit yanked tight, and I screamed again. "The exertion. You came?"

"Yes, yes—"

"How many times?"

"Once. Once. It isn't stopping."

"You feel like you are still coming, Goddess?"

I nodded helplessly as he continued to thrust, slow, steady pushes of his cock inside of me. I had been surprised each time it had fit last night, and now, I felt every vein of it, every bump, my cunt's sensitivity taken to the utmost so I felt even when the head of him pounded into my womb.

Dizziness washed through me, consumed me, became me, a collision of sensation and desire and his expert unwinding of my body.

"Come again," he told me, gruff. "Come on me."

I shook my head. "It's too much, Hephaestus—I can't."

"You can, Aphrodite." He dragged his hand up my stomach, between my breasts, up my arms, to where my wrists hung in the manacles. I hadn't noticed they were getting sore until he unlocked them and let my body fall, pinned between his and the forge. "You want me to teach you? Then come when I tell you to. Trust that I know what your body needs. I can see it in your face, Goddess—I can see it in your needy, plump lips. *Come on me.*"

He thrust his hips forward and up, lifting me against the forge, pushing the clamp against my clit, and I shrieked. Another orgasm broke through, fighting the lingering remnants of the last until I was a living war of overlapping pleasure.

Hephaestus grabbed one breast and undid a clamp. The pleasure peeked and my shriek turned garbled as he sucked that nipple into his mouth, tonguing the sore bud in apology. He repeated it on the other, and *aftershocks* was too insufficient a word—they were full quakes still, jarring explosions of pleasure that had me writhing and fighting for air.

"Breathe, Goddess," he told me again, and he undid the clamp on my clit.

Vivid and pulsing, one final orgasm ripped through my body, pushing my very being out of this shell and into some kind of rainbow-streaked ether.

I was vaguely aware of kissing him, of anchoring my arms around his neck and fucking him where he stood, hips rolling, cunt swallowing his cock in greedy thrusts. This pleasure was too much, too *big* for just my body; I needed him to feel it, I needed to ruin him as perfectly as he had ruined me.

He spun our bodies and slammed me onto one of his worktables, tools scattering, metals clanking to the floor. We were a cyclone, hands and ankles and teeth, scratches and bites and bruising lunges. The cradle of my hips fit around his as though it had been sculpted to hold him, and in all the presumed filth of the dirt and sweat on our bodies, nothing felt as filthy as the way he grabbed my neck and forced my head to the table and snarled into my ear, "Do you want my mark on you, Goddess?"

"Yes, yes—"

He reared back, yanking his cock out of me, and pumped it into his hand over my stomach. He came with a tear of that beautiful rage and passion, his seed spilling across the apron and my belly, up my breasts.

I did not give him time to come down; I hooked my hand around his neck and demanded that his face be near mine as I arched my back, showing him what he had done in the orange glow of the furnace.

"I love you," I told him. "I love you, Hephaestus, I—"

He kissed me, swallowing that declaration, and reared up to

stare down at me, at my body.

His fingerprints were on my breasts, on my arms. His come was on my stomach, smeared white.

He panted, and I saw him take stock of what he had done, the delirium fading from him.

He kissed me, dragging his fingers across my scalp, seizing hold of my hair. "I love you," he said into me. "I love you, too."

18

Hephaestus

We created, in the stifled halls of Olympus, a heaven. Aphrodite helped me make dozens of enchanted items. We passed them to Thalia, who distributed them to nymphs and demigods and more.

I taught Aphrodite how to work the forge. I watched her body strain with effort and sculpt beneath the weight and when I could take no longer the fact that she was *real*, and *here*, and *mine*, I would press her to the forge and fuck her in my home, make her scream until her pleasure wrung out both her body and mine.

Stories came to us through servants and gossip—gods at orgies flung across the room. A goddess who couldn't stop vomiting. Others who suffered the ill effects of enchanted items on bearers who did not want to be touched, until I knew that the whole of the mountain was in a tizzy with not knowing why their callous rules had been upended.

Between that and having Aphrodite's soft presence in my forge, I was oblivious in my joy. Even when we went to the orb and checked in on the war, I could not be unhappy that it continued. Greece made no progress against Troy; Troy made no progress in removing Greece. It kept Ares away, and though Aphrodite bore no small amount of guilt from it, we did what we could to alleviate the burden on the mortals.

And she let me bring her back to our forge, where we worked, and created beautiful things, and were happy.

"I know why the other gods treat you so poorly," she said one day. How many had it been since our wedding? If time had been meaningless on Olympus before, it was nonexistent now.

"Oh?" I barely thought about the other gods now. She was my whole reality.

"They are jealous of you."

I gave her a look over our worktable. One of flat shock. "Obviously. I have *you*."

She grinned. "No." My wife waved at the forge. "You constantly create *new* in a world that is trapped by the *same*. They're threatened by you. They envy you."

I sat back, eyes flitting over her, silhouetted by the orange coals.

I hadn't thought of it like that before. That I was the one god capable of eternally creating new. Of *creating* at all.

And now I had the Goddess of Beauty.

Skill and beauty.

We needed nothing else.

My stool scraped against the floor as I rose and bent forward to catch her lips with mine. I would never tire of kissing her, of the gentle sound of enjoyment she made each time, as if the taste of me was as addictive as the taste of her.

"I still think they're most jealous that I have you," I said with a grin.

She batted my shoulder and bent back to work.

In all my centuries in Olympus, all the lessons I had learned the hard way, I should have been more suspicious of our uninterrupted joy.

And I should have heeded Aphrodite's words as foretelling: they were threatened by me. Had always been.

But for the first time in the whole of my existence, I was *happy*. I was the god of skill, and I wanted nothing more than to be skilled at joy, and so I, stupidly, gave into that.

But I knew well that the root of Olympus was not joy.

It was pride.

I had been a threat to the other gods when I was a recluse and a monster. Now that I had a joyous marriage, and, most ominously, created enchanted items we spread like a disease beset on the worst of the gods? I had blossomed from an annoyance to a true, hulking menace.

And now.

I had something to lose when they came for me.

Something more vital than a jilted lover, or my own limbs.

19

Aphrodite

"This should be the last of it," said Hephaestus, stacking a final ring in a basket of other jewelry.

We had supplied countless such protective enchantments throughout Olympus. And the only proof of the changes we enacted came through rumors or Thalia's tales—I had not ventured to Olympus's gatherings since my wedding, to the point that the whole wide fog of this mountain was beginning to feel more and more a dream. This was the reality I had forged here, one of crafting and joy and *him*—the changes I brought to Olympus beyond were not for me, but for others.

And it was changing. Thalia was lighter each time I saw her. She was buoyant.

"And then I have more orders from Zeus." He sat at his worktable and looked over a scroll that had arrived not long ago, born from the messenger god, who had tried to peek past Hephaestus's shoulders into the room—*"You keep her locked up, Soot God! Let's have a look—"* until my husband had slammed the door in his face. "More weapons."

My gut twisted as I drew a blanket over the basket. "How

long has it been in mortal years now?"

"Nearly ten." Hephaestus looked up at me. I felt his weight on the side of my face. It lingered, and I knew he wanted me to look at him; I couldn't bring myself to.

Finally, he put his fingers under my chin, pulled my gaze to his.

"You will look in on the orb after you make this delivery to Thalia?" he asked.

I nodded.

"Stay with your nymphs for a while. They lift your spirits."

"You lift my spirits more."

"Ah, but I cannot be your sole focus. You have too much to give, Goddess."

I frowned in his hand. "Did what Hermes said get to you? Do not let it. I am happy here, Hephaestus. Deliriously so. Need I show you how much?"

I tried for a sly smile, but that number beat in my mind. *Ten years.*

Ten long years of a mortal war.

Ten years of every god being involved in some way, until Olympus buzzed as much with rumors of the war as with stories of gods being affected by errant pieces of jewelry.

How many lives had been lost by now? I had poured out what beauty and love I could, and while Paris and Helen remained untouched, I did not know what else could be done. Hephaestus tried to assure me, but more and more, I felt that love wasn't enough.

And it terrified me.

For if the Goddess of Love could not end a mortal war, what hope did I have of protecting my own love?

I leaned into Hephaestus's warm palm, pressing it to my face, eyes shutting before he could read too deeply into my gnawing fear. "I will return shortly."

"Not too shortly." His thumb moved on the pillow of my cheek. "I would see you smile when you return, Aphrodite. Do something joyous with your nymphs. Please."

I kissed his hand. "Very well. Since you asked so graciously."

He grinned. "I will graciously ask other things of you tonight."

He started to turn for his table. I caught his face in my hands and bent down to where he was seated before me. The size of him next to the size of me meant even seated he was nearly at my height, and I had not far to go to kiss him.

His fingers hooked into the strophion I had on already. I held there for a beat too long, drawing strength from the smell of him, sweat and iron, from the heat of him, the bulk of his sturdiness.

"Aphrodite?" Concern tinged his voice.

I pulled back and shook my head. "The war will end soon, won't it?"

His face darkened. "Yes." His eyes dropped to the strophion. "And then we shall face a different sort of war."

When Ares returned.

When he made good on his threats towards me.

When he discovered how the game of Olympus had been reset in his absence.

Once the war stopped drawing the focus of all the gods, would they turn their attention more pointedly towards the source of the enchanted items?

They would come for us. Wouldn't they?

I lifted the basket, steadying under the weight of my strophion, and left my forge with a last, backwards glance at

Hephaestus, at his worktable, lit by the orange of the coals, his sweaty face soft and loving as he watched me go.

I went to the orb room, basket in tow. We had quickly discovered that that was one of the best rooms to pass off any enchanted items—never were other gods there to see us. Between that and my suite, we were ghosts, slipping violent rings and cuffs and strophions to Thalia.

We were reforming Olympus to be beautiful for all. According to what my nymphs said, they no longer feared the mere act of walking down halls, and had even begun partaking in things without recoil—listening to music performances, indulging in feasts. Others were following suit, and while that energy shift alone was addictive and infusing, ever I felt a foreboding shadow.

Was it truly this easy to bring beauty to the most corrupt place?

As I pushed into the orb room, that soft blue glow waiting for me, I couldn't tell whether the prickle on the back of my neck was from my usual worry, or something new.

A shadow peeled out of the edge of the room and I jumped.

It was Thalia. "Goddess! Forgive me. Forgive me, but I—" She staggered forward a step, her movements jerky, panicked.

"Are you all right?"

"No, no, Goddess. Did you speak with Hephaestus?"

"I just left him."

"How long ago? I came just from him with news—news on the items you made."

My eyes shot to the closed door. "What news? He did not say."

"No, you would have missed me there—oh, Goddess, it is

horrible!" Thalia's hands flew to her cheeks and she reeled, eyes widening.

I set down the basket, arms going out should I need to catch her. "Thalia! What is wrong? What—"

"The items you made! Some have started to—have started to *turn* on their bearers!" Thalia's face grayed. "Demigods electrocuted by their own strophions—Goddess, do you understand?"

"Do I—no, that is not the enchantment Hephaestus laid! Thalia—"

"I saw it!" Thalia rushed to me, tugging at my strophion. "Please, Goddess—do not let it hurt you!"

She was sobbing.

Full, heaving sobs, the likes of which I had never seen on her, and the sight sent me into such a flustered horror that I relented, helping her unfasten the strophion, letting it drop to the floor with a clank.

"All right, Thalia—I am fine, I am—"

"*No*, Goddess!" She screamed. Bright, piercing, and she fell to her knees, her whole body trembling, hands tugging at her hair, tears staining her skirt.

I started to bend down to her. Started to reach for her—

That sense of dread clutched at me.

And I knew.

I knew as I stood, and turned, and my eyes locked on the far, dark corner of the room.

It had been a trick.

My breath came in tight, heated gasps as Ares stepped into the blue glow of the orb. He was in his war clothes, gore-smeared and sweat-drenched as though he had stepped fresh from battle, his eyes bright with blood mania.

I didn't move. Carefully neutral. I was not a threat. I was

not—

Ares took a step, and I grabbed for the strophion. My hands were sweaty—I snatched it and dove for the door, struggling to get it on, but he was fast, faster than I, and in two leaps he closed the distance.

His body slammed into mine, pinning me to the door. The strophion was not fastened.

I screamed.

Hephaestus was too far away.

No one would be nearby, not this room.

Still, I shrieked again, and Thalia, still on the floor, wailed and rolled forward, head in her hands, succumbed to pain.

"What did you do to her?" I demanded, bucking back against Ares.

He ran his nose up the side of my face. "Oh, Beauty, I missed you."

"Let me *go*. Now."

"Or what? You'll get your nymph to fight me? No, I don't think she will. Your *husband* isn't the only one who can enchant items, you know."

I went still. I couldn't twist to look at him, flattened to the door like this, but I willed my body to calm, to not waste energy, not now. "What did you—"

He spun me around, hand tangled up in my hair. It twisted with such force that I screamed again and he dropped me to my knees, the strophion clattering away as I reached for his grip on my hair.

I saw Thalia before me, weeping.

Dangling around her throat was the necklace Ares had given me as a wedding gift.

"You were meant to put it on, Beauty," Ares stated above

me. "But here I take a much-needed reprieve from war to find out that the Soot God has not only made you his whore, but you seem *eager* for it? And the stories my siblings have told me! Of nymphs suddenly capable of shooting *lightning* and inducing *pain.* No, the mortal war can wait. What you did to Apollo could have passed—but my *brother,*" he twisted his wrist, wrenching my hair tighter, and I arched back with a piercing wail, "has been staging a coup, it seems, while we have all been distracted."

"No—" I tried, but Ares clamped his hand around my throat and pinched down.

"No, no, Beauty—you do not get to defend him. He has you utterly under his own enchantments, hasn't he? He set these rules. I am merely following." He nudged Thalia with his foot. She was sobbing quietly now, holding herself, rocking back and forth. My heart broke—what had he done to her under the influence of that necklace? "He forced me to this extreme. I never meant for you to see this side of war, Beauty." Ares lifted me to my feet, turning me to face him, his hand still vice-pinching my throat so I felt all my blood begin to surge to my face, heating it, choking me with each throb. "This is the most unfortunate of the games we play on Olympus. You should not have to bear witness to such messy business, but he has made you the symbol of our victory. And now, that victory is mine."

He marched from the room, dragging me as nothing more than a limp doll. Terror surged through me and I kicked and roiled, but I was nothing to him, weightless and choking. I could not die from lack air; my vision heaved in and out and I stayed helplessly conscious, watching as Thalia wept on the floor of the orb room, as the heavy iron door banged shut behind us, as lights passed over Ares and he hauled me up, up, up into Olympus.

Farther from the forge than I had ever been.

20

Hephaestus

The heat of my forge grew, suddenly, cold.

I shrugged at it and cast my gaze around. The coals hadn't died; what had—

My mind raced through the time. I had been at work on Zeus's order for the war—more bolts, weaponry, all enchanted—but Aphrodite should have been back by now? How long had it been?

I shot to my feet.

Nothing had changed. But everything had.

A shift in the air. A brush of prickles running up my arm.

I holstered a hammer in my apron's belt. Thought better of it, and grabbed more weapons, things I had honestly never used before. But I was driven by something dark and growing, and it pushed me out the door, iron boots clanging on the floor.

The halls of Olympus washed over me in a blur. I thought of how I should have passed her, maybe, laughing with Thalia; but the deep, dark instinct told me I wouldn't, hefting into terror until I reached the orb room. Why not her suite? But I knew—I knew, a pull in my gut, a screaming sense of *wrong*—

I opened the door to see Thalia on the floor by the orb, arms around her torso, staring blankly at the far wall.

Next to her was the basket of enchanted objects Aphrodite had delivered.

And—

My wife's strophion. Opened. Not on her body.

I bolted inside, eyes snapping around, but she wasn't here. "Thalia! What happened?"

The nymph didn't respond. I knelt before her, but her eyes were sightless on the middle space, her mouth parted, lax.

Something had been done to her.

I recognized this enchantment, and it sent a brutal chill through my veins.

I had *refused* to make an enchantment like this, centuries ago. Ares had come up with it.

He had sneered as he'd asked. *"What if you make it so the wearer becomes utterly submissive? Obedient in every way?"*

I thought of my missing materials. The gold, the enchantment dust.

When had I left my forge unattended? But I did, often; any time, he could have entered. Any time, he could have made something—

My eyes cut over Thalia's body, searching for gold—I spotted it instantly, a pendant on her neck.

I ripped it off and stuffed it in my apron pocket.

Thalia gasped breath and rocked backwards, that gust of air releasing in a scream.

Her eyes fixed on me and she buckled. "He made me do it, God Hephaestus! Forgive me, forgive me—" She hiccuped in her terror, and her eyes rounded. "Oh no, no—God—help her, help her, *go—*"

"Go where? Where did he—"

"Ares," she coughed, gagging, and sobbed anew, her red cheeks reddening all the more, such deep sorrow in her that I feared she'd collapse. "Ares has her. God Hephaestus, please—"

I snatched Aphrodite's strophion from the floor. "Go to her suite," I told Thalia, and I took off, needing nothing more.

My mind shuttered. Focused.

Ares had found us out. The enchantments, the strophion. He'd returned.

Panic wrestled for control of my body, but I beat it down, fuming at it, at myself. I felt a repeat of years ago, running to his room in a frantic tear. Only this time, my feet were already ruined, and each step recoiled through me, my rage tinged with memories of Cabeiro falling—and before, how she had been once Ares had caught her, terror fragrant and consuming.

Only now, it was Aphrodite, and the sheer flash of imagining her in Cabeiro's place had me breaking into a desperate run, flying through the halls of this accursed place.

How long had it been since he'd taken her?

I couldn't answer that. I couldn't *think*, not with her gone, not with her in his hands.

All I knew was that once I found him. Once I had her back.

I would make the God of War bleed.

21

Aphrodite

Ares hauled me somewhere high in Olympus. We passed others; I saw them in dizzying flashes through my air-deprived mind. None intervened. Some laughed. One, a soldier, fell in step with Ares, and he ordered the demigod on guard as he dragged me into a room and slammed the door.

Finally, he released me, dumping me in the center of a massive room. A window billowed salty air, and as I gripped my fingers into a rug beneath me, I fought to breathe that air in the absence of his hand.

He barely let me take a single shaking inhale before he seized my hair again and heaved me to my feet.

I whimpered, grabbing his wrist, tears dripping down my face.

"It didn't have to be like this, Beauty," Ares told me. He tossed me again, and this time I landed on something soft, cushioned—a bed.

I rubbed my throat, coughed, glaring at him as he stood before me. "You prefer it this way," I managed, garbled.

He cut a wicked grin. "Am I so transparent? Although," he worked at the buckle on his blood-streaked breastplate, "the protective enchantments do pose an interesting new obstacle. And you know how we love anything *new*."

I managed to right my breathing, to center my spinning vision. His room was large, done in violent browns and reds. I spotted the window, but we were too high for it to be useful—and I remembered Hephaestus's story, his fall, and I shuddered—and I saw the closed door.

Ares turned to set his breastplate on a mannequin. "It might be a fun addition to the orgies, hm? Adding in those enchantments to—"

I launched from the bed while his back was to me.

I got three steps. Maybe four.

His grip snapped around my arm and he let my own momentum yank my feet from beneath me before he slammed me to my back on the floor.

I cried out, the breath knocked from me, and he bent down, watching me writhe.

Ares tipped his head, hands between his bent legs, bare chest cut with muscles and streaked with war dirt.

"Will you fight the whole while? I expected different from the Goddess of *Love*."

I pushed up onto my elbows, hair hanging over my face in matted tangles, tears and sweat and spit streaked across my face. "I . . . love . . . Hephaestus," I choked, body ringing with pain.

Ares rolled his eyes. "What a powerful enchantment he has on you for you to believe that. What item is it, I wonder?" His gaze roved over me. "I shall find it. You'll thank me when it's removed, Beauty. Oh, will you *thank* me."

Again, he grabbed my hair.

Again, he dragged me to his bed and tossed me there.

This time, he didn't back away. I crawled against the bedding and he knotted his grip into the hem of my gown and *pulled*, and the fabric tore, much as my gown had at Peleus and Thetis's wedding.

Horror washed in a cold sheet over me, but it was too late—I scrambled, seeking something to cover myself, but the blankets were knotted, too thick.

I was naked before him. Under his probing, intense gaze as he knelt on the end of the bed.

But he wasn't staring at me with that usual hunger. He was looking me over, surveying my breasts, my belly; he grabbed my legs and spread me and I screamed, then he flipped me, and I scrambled away.

"There is nothing," he stated, a flare of anger tingeing his voice. "What enchantment does he have on you? What item do you have of his?"

"*Nothing,*" I snarled at him, crawling, crawling—

But he kept a grip on my ankle and yanked me back to him. I spun, gasping, and the look on him now was possessive, the beginnings of understanding.

That I was not under an enchantment when I had said I loved Hephaestus.

That I was not fighting Ares because of magic, but because of my own choice.

So I said it again. "I love him. I love him."

If I said it enough, it would save me—the words were a lifeline, a call to him, *I love him, I love*—

Ares scoffed. His grip bore down on my ankle. "No one could love something like *that*. I broke him. I know how ruined he

163

is."

"He isn't ruined," I couldn't control my breathing, panting too hard, more and more aware of my defenseless against Ares's rising realizations. "He's beautiful. Even before I loved him, he was beautiful. You're too shallow and stupid to appreciate him."

Ares dove at me.

I screamed, throat tearing to bleeding, and his hand clamped around my neck, pushing me into the bedding. His other hand roamed, groping me, the furious look in his eyes contrasting with his swollen, snarling grin.

That immobilizing panic grabbed me again. Even if I could have fought back, my body didn't listen, my will pounding heedlessly on a closed door.

"Love or not," he said to me, forcing my legs to part, grabbing my cunt as he once had, and terror bucked through me, "I still claim his victory."

I tried to scream again. His grip on my throat compressed, and the light of his room shifted and swirled in my dizzying eyes, colors in teal and pink and gold.

Some part of my breaking mind noted it with a flare of hope. *There is beauty here,* it said. *Even now.*

But what could beauty do for me?

22

Hephaestus

There was a soldier standing outside Ares's room. He looked at my approach and sneered, but as I did not slow, a full-out, barreling run, the demigod's face drooped, then paled.

"Ares—" he started to call out, but I grabbed the soldier by his breastplate and heaved him, bodily, down the hall, the metal of his armor banging off marble and cracking a table and shuddering the very walls with my rage.

Within the room, there was silence.

That silence was more horrifying, more destructively consuming, than anything had been yet, and I faced the door, reared back, and kicked.

It splintered inward with a shattering crack beneath my iron boot and my eyes snapped immediately to Ares's bed.

He was over her.

Kneeling over top of her; there, her legs beneath his, thrashing—

I was across the room before Ares had even glanced back. He still had on his pleated soldier's kilt, but that detail only vaguely registered; his hand was around her throat, his other lodged in her cunt, and I was a beast, truly, utterly, I had never been made such a creature as this moment.

One of the weapons I had grabbed—an immobilizing net—came into my hands.

I wanted him to know I was dismembering him, limb by limb, and be unable to stop it.

Ares twisted towards me, but I was a blur—the net cracked out, whipped around his torso, and I heaved backwards, flinging him to the floor.

He went immediately limp, arms strapped to his chest, the net expanding in its enchantment until it encircled his entire body.

An axe slipped into my hand.

We would see if his god-might could mend his body back from pieces. If it could pull in his blood once it had been painted across the floor. If—

"Hephaestus," Aphrodite sobbed, her voice roughened and I could not fall apart yet, she needed me, she was here and alive and she *needed me*—

I scooped her into my arms, unable to hold her trembling body tight enough; I wanted to press her inside of me, cocoon her in safety, and she scrambled against me, sobbing, her whole frame quivering with the force of her unwinding.

My eyes dropped to Ares. Immobile. Taken by surprise. For the first time in our existences, I had the upper hand on him.

But Aphrodite continued to shake, her bare skin prickling and ice cold, and I took off out of the room at a run.

23

Aphrodite

Hephaestus bolted back down through Olympus. I faded in and out, half from pain, half from shock, until I came to at the slamming of the forge's door, the massive bolt dropping over it.

He hefted me into one arm and began to drag other things in front of the door. A table. A barrel of metals that he effortlessly moved with one hand, putting up a blockade, and I wondered, vaguely, if it would be enough to stop Ares, to stop Zeus if he wished to enter.

What would happen when Ares broke free?

Could we hide in this forge forever?

Yes, yes, I tried to whimper it. I never wanted to leave again. I never would, strophion or not; I would be here, with him, two recluses, two outcasts—

A sob sprang through me, thoroughly defeated. It came from all my suppressed fear, the waiting stalk of terror that I had known this was coming; from the pain I had caused on Earth with the war, those mistakes demanding repayment from me now. I fell apart in Hephaestus's arms and he dove across the

167

forge, kicked into the bathing room, and leapt with me, him fully clothed, into the sweltering water of the mountain-heated bath.

"Aphrodite," he said my name, a gentle prod. I couldn't stop crying, letting the lull of the water lap at my skin, the skin that Ares had touched, that he had—

I reared up to kiss Hephaestus, needing his mouth on me, needing it *now*. He relented instantly, rocking into me, but when he tried to pull back, I gripped onto him and didn't let him. I needed his touch all over, needed his rough hands to scrub away Ares, needed, needed, I was all need only, sobbing, messy desperation, and I broke away with a startled wail, slipping and wobbling to the side of the bathing pool where I held there, hand to my mouth, gasping for breath.

"Aphrodite," Hephaestus said again, and his voice was pinched with tears. "Did he—"

"No," I managed. No, he had tried to make me want it first, a final claim at his feeble victory.

The pause that followed made way for my shaky gulps at air, the beating of the pool's water on the stones, the grate of Hephaestus's restrained breaths.

"What will happen?" I asked him as I once had. Seeking his guidance on all things Olympus. Relying on him and him alone for protection.

"Ares will take it to Zeus," Hephaestus said.

"He accused you of staging a coup with your enchantments," I whispered, eyes on the dark water.

There was another pause. Enough that I looked up and watched Hephaestus sink back against the edge, his eyes unfocused.

"I have been making weapons to hurt gods," he said absently.

"To unseat the balance of power. In a way . . . he is right."

"Will Zeus agree?" I twisted to him, shaking again, even with the natural heat of this bath.

Hephaestus shrugged. "He may laugh it off—none of these enchantments truly *defeated* a god, merely wounded them temporarily. But if Ares is furious enough, he could rile Zeus."

"And then?" I barely heard my own voice. "What would they do?"

How could an immortal be punished? I had seen the shade of bloodlust on Hephaestus as he'd looked at the immobile Ares, but what could truly be done?

Hephaestus looked up at me. "You will not worry about that."

And I dove forward, frantic; of all the things that had happened, that look of defeat in his eyes was the most unraveling.

"We can leave," I said into him.

His arms came around me, his apron darkened in the water, his clothes soaked through. "And go where?"

"Earth. Hide among the mortals."

"Zeus would find us."

"So we bow to his judgment?" I jerked back, tears falling anew. "We tried to make this place *safe* and *good*, and we are to merely wait for the whims of these arrogant gods? What good is our station here if we are as helpless as mortals?" I was sobbing again, asking the same questions I felt I had been asking for my entire existence. "Hephaestus—we cannot continue like this—we *cannot*—I'm so sorry. I'm so sorry, Hephaestus—"

He yanked me back to him, but not before I saw the tears in his own eyes, and that unwound me even more.

"I do not regret it," he said into the bend of my shoulder. "Do you understand that? I would not change a thing we have done."

"I have endangered you. I forced you to do this—"

"I willingly did it. I should have done it sooner. I am shamed only that I did not think to attempt change in Olympus until you, but it is because of your generosity and fairness and love that I was able to foresee a better existence at all." His grip on me pulled tighter, crushing me to him; I felt the same, that I could not get close enough. "You came as a being of love in a callous place, and your every moment here should have been heralded as the dawning of a new age for gods to build purpose into their meaningless eternities by your example. You are my forever, Aphrodite, my destiny and my soul, and I will stand firm by your side, fighting until my last immortal breath, until Olympus sees in you the hope that I feel every moment in your presence."

I sobbed into him, sinking into his words, the love that poured off of him in waves. How could he still believe any promise in what I had to offer? We saw over and over again how little love could truly do against the destructive force of the other gods. And we felt it, now, coming for us, the repercussions of our love in this mountain.

We were trapped. So brief our joy had been, and it would be eviscerated by shortsighted, weak-willed gods who sought only to break their own boredom. They were petty and stupid and I had been a fool to think I could change things here—me, just another new thing in a world of things, what prayer had I ever truly had to make Olympus better?

I clung to Hephaestus in the scorching water, feeling the shudder of his inhale as he suppressed his tears, fighting to be strong for me.

His lips pressed to my bare shoulder, and that was all I

needed.

I grabbed through the water at his clothes, and he moved, wordless, eyes shut, sweat slicking with the steam of the pool and our own exhales. His cock sprang free in the water and I sheathed it in me in one motion that had him giving a tight, mangled whimper, his hand clasping the back of my neck.

"Aphrodite," he whispered, and that was all, just my name, a plea, a promise he had said dozens of times, and I leaned my forehead to his as I ground my hips up and down his cock.

The feel of him centered me. Completed me. My body had been made to form with his and I kept my pace slow, intentional, feeling every thrust, every pulse, skin scalded to raw in the water.

All of this had happened because of me. I had asked him to make the strophions for my nymphs. I had opened his eyes to the idea of fighting back. I had taken my purpose of love and tried to reform this broken mountain into something beautiful.

I refused to play the games the other gods did, and so they would ever have that power over me of being ruthless. Love would always lose against their pride.

But they loved games so much—perhaps there was a way I could finally give them what they wanted, if it meant sparing Hephaestus.

He would refuse. I did not dare mention that spark of idea—he would react how I would if he had suggested sacrificing himself to spare me. So I just rode him, rode him until my body stopped shaking with fear and started to shake with release, his own building with his fingers digging into my hips, until we both came with soft, distorted cries, and my sorrow and terror subsided into an echoing resolve.

Whatever Zeus decided. Whatever Ares pushed at us.

It would not touch Hephaestus.

He was the lone spot of goodness in this mountain, and as the Goddess of Beauty, it was my destiny, my duty, my honor, to protect him.

24

Hephaestus

The light catcher over our bed hued the room in gentle pricks of blue, and I let my eyes drift out in that beauty as she lay on my chest, her legs knotted with mine. She had stopped shaking, dressed now in one of her simple gowns, but I did not think she was asleep. We lay in tense silence, both of us, I knew, waiting, listening, bracing.

And so when a knock came on the door—not the main door to my forge, but the one to this room—we both went rigid.

I bolted upright and pushed her behind me, but she grabbed my face and kissed me, lingering in that act. I breathed her in, breathing, breathing, that sweet vanilla warmth, the fire in her eyes, the passion she emitted and stoked.

She had asked what they could do to punish a god. She had not been here long enough to know all of Olympus's most brutal history.

But I did.

I knew what happened to gods who disobeyed in ways that truly upset Zeus.

Towards the beginning of Earth, a god had stolen fire to

give to the first mortals; he hadn't wanted them to shiver quite so much. Zeus had him strapped to a rock on the shoreline in a hidden cove, where daily, an eagle pecked out his liver and it regrew through his god-might. He had been there for centuries.

I had not pieced together the gravity of what I had done in making these protective enchantments until she'd said that word, *coup*, and I had felt the snap of repercussions spin on me.

All I could see now was Aphrodite strapped to a rock, in some hidden cove that Zeus would keep from me, sentenced to forever be ripped apart where I could not reach her. He would know with one glance that hurting her would be my worst punishment, and try as I did to school my face as I approached the door, I couldn't.

If they touched her.

If they used her to punish me for what I had done—what *I* had done; she would be blameless in this—then something would be born in me that could not be suppressed.

Mortals said that the monsters that stalked Earth—hydras and harpies and gorgons and more—came from the destruction of gods.

I wondered what monster would come from me if they hurt her.

I set my jaw, feeling the stiffness of my drying tunic against my chest as I breathed deep, and opened the door.

Hermes stood just outside.

My eyes shot to the main door to my forge. It was still blocked by piled objects.

I gave him a withering glare.

He nodded behind him, at the far window that looked down

at the sea. "Your window is open. I can fly."

I said nothing.

He sighed. "Zeus demands your presence in the banquet hall. Both of you." To his credit, he did not try to look past me, into the bedroom.

I almost refused. It was there, a curse and a shout, that Hermes could tell Zeus to shove his own fist up his ass—but I would not make this worse.

My nod came slow. "We will appear."

Hermes hesitated. "Those objects. That was you?"

Again, I said nothing.

"Hm," was all he said.

I frowned at the thoughtfulness in his eyes. He bore none of the anger I knew was awaiting me from Zeus. Why?

But Hermes lifted into the air and was gone, flashing back out through the window.

I turned to see Aphrodite up already, working her hair back, straightening her gown. She put on her strophion again.

"I am ready," she said, her eyes on the floor, a strange sort of calm in her leveled words.

A kind of premonition had my gut twisting. "You can stay here. I can—"

Now she looked at me, a glare. "This is not yours to bear alone. You swore to me that I would be yours forever—so *all* of you will walk into that hall, because we are one."

I shot towards her. "And that is what terrifies me."

It came on a surge of tears. A rush and shudder of agony.

My eyes snapped shut, but tears fell, and I hung my head on a gasp at air.

Her palm cupped my jaw. I forced my eyes open, looking at her through a blur, and she managed a smile, her thumb stroking over my bottom lip.

"You will protect what is yours," she whispered. "And I will protect what is mine."

Briefly, I saw myself bolting her into this room. They could not hurt her if they could not reach her.

But I wilted into her touch, kissed her palm, ran those kisses up her arm until I gathered her into me and held her.

"I love you," I promised her.

She pressed her face to the side of mine. "And I love you, Hephaestus."

25

Aphrodite

He kept his arm around me as we walked up through the marbled halls of Olympus, and as we approached the banquet room, hearing the chatter and murmur of a crowd, his grip drew tighter, until I truly believed we were one being as we stepped into the archway.

The crowd's murmurs fell to utter silence.

Gods and demigods and nymphs were here, the swell of the crowd that had been present for Peleus and Thetis's wedding, back before the war had dispersed so many to Earth. But the energy of the room now was not one of half-bored revelry; drink still flowed, and the faux sky was still lovely, but the moment Hephaestus and I appeared, eyes shot to us with predatory interest.

I was so used to that look from them now. I wanted to yawn, as they did, to show my disinterest in their petty games. But my stomach was a knot of terror, even with their inability to show anything new, and as Hephaestus guided me into the room, I kept my eyes on the line of the pillars across from us, not noting who was present.

The crowd parted, creating a short path to the far edge, where a massive throne had been arranged. Gilded gold and set with rubies and diamonds, the chair towered over everyone else, lifting Zeus so he sat in his customary place: above all.

Hephaestus had made that chair. I recognized the touch of his craftsmanship, the care he'd put into sculpting ivy along the arms and how he'd set each stone with added flares of enchanted dust to make them glow softly.

I gripped Hephaestus's arm around my waist, staying off a whimper.

We stopped before Zeus. He clutched the armrests of his throne, the only sign of his displeasure a slight curl to his nostril.

"Hephaestus," Zeus said, and I wanted to beg attention on me instead. "You are accused of creating all manner of jewelry that intentionally harm and weaken gods. Do you have anything to say for yourself?"

"I did so," he began, and I felt the rumble of his voice where my shoulder was pressed to his chest, "to help other occupants of Olympus. Others, God-King, who were created by you and so too deserve your aid, do they not?"

Zeus's lip curled. "In the chaos that has been Greece's war with Troy, you saw an opening in our distraction. You have always hated us, haven't you, Hephaestus? I did not see the depth of your hatred. I should have."

A thought occurred to me: had Zeus felt the effect of one of our enchanted items? Had he tried to force himself on a nymph or other, and been blasted with lightning or sickened?

I would have laughed, had his glare not been fixed so fumingly on Hephaestus.

"I do not hate you," Hephaestus said, sounding winded.

178

"Long have I wanted Olympus to be fairer. Righter. This was meant to enact that."

"You would change us?"

"You do love change." The moment he said that, I felt his wince.

The room gasped.

Zeus rocked forward. "You betrayed your own kind!"

"I leveled the field," Hephaestus said, his grip on me shaking; he was fighting for calm.

"And I will level it further." He nodded to someone in the crowd. It parted, and demigod soldiers approached, arrayed in resplendent gold armor.

At their lead was Ares.

I did not get a chance to cry out. The soldiers descended on us and Hephaestus pushed me away with such force that I stumbled and tripped to the floor and spun to see the soldiers grab him.

Ares smirked as his demigods kicked my husband to his knees.

"You are useful, Hephaestus, but I have let your leash grow too lax," Zeus said. He rose from his throne. "Remove his arm."

I threw a sickened look up at Zeus, towering over me.

He wasn't watching me. He was glaring at Hephaestus.

"It will be reattached," Zeus said. "And taken apart. Again, and again, until you remember whom you serve."

Hephaestus writhed, but he submitted, going limp in the soldiers' hands, and I saw a wash of relief over him.

Relief that they had not gone for me.

As Ares drew a sword from his belt, the silver blade flashing starlight in the expanse of the banquet hall, I screamed.

"Do not touch him!"

The room's tension sharpened.

And pivoted to me.

Hephaestus gave me a pleading, dismayed look, but I scrambled to my feet and swung on Zeus.

"Do not touch him," I commanded.

Zeus stared at me for one shocked moment.

Then he bellowed a cruel laugh.

"Do not worry for your place here, Goddess," he said with a dismissive bat of his hand. "Ares—she is yours."

"One moment," he said with a vicious grin and reared his sword high. A sword that Hephaestus had made.

The demigods stretched Hephaestus's arm out.

I choked, a cry mangling in my closing throat.

Hephaestus writhed now, terror graying him as he looked at me, his iron boots slipping on the marbled floor.

"STOP!"

But the sword swung, glinting off the faux light, and I screamed again.

Ares brought the blade down, hard, on Hephaestus's shoulder.

One blow would not slice off this god's arm, thickened from work and strain, and Ares dragged the blade free from the cut it had made. Wickedly deep, the gash spurted thick red blood that sprayed across the demigods, across the floor, across Hephaestus.

He didn't cry out. He panted and gritted his teeth and looked at me in silent begging, to run, to leave him, to *stop*.

I couldn't.

I couldn't think past the sight of his blood, the deepness of that cut, how Ares would go deeper, deeper, over and over until Zeus was satisfied. I could *feel* that pain as though the sword had pummeled straight into my own soul, and as Ares lifted his bloodied sword again, I dove in front of him.

The sword arched, but it stopped, Ares's body yanking up short to retract as his eyes focused on me.

He was livid.

"Move her," he demanded, and other demigods started for me.

"I will be yours," I told him. "I won't fight. Yours entirely, forever. You like games?" I was talking fast, manic; my sandals were standing in a pool of my husband's blood. "All of you. You love games so much? I have one you can play."

I looked back at Zeus.

Ares and his demigods held.

"What game, Goddess?" Zeus asked, his deep voice rumbling across the silent crowd.

Hephaestus, behind me, made a choked, garbled sound of protest. "No—Aphrodite—"

"I will go with Ares. I will be his. Hephaestus will stop making enchanted items and Olympus will return to the way it was before I arrived."

"If?" Zeus tipped his head.

"If Paris and Helen lose this war." Saying it tugged at the very base of my soul.

The banquet hall hung in considering silence. Some were shocked, maybe; I couldn't tell. The whole of my focus was on Zeus, on Ares, on the sound of Hephaestus's panicked gasps behind me.

"Aphrodite," he pleaded, and I heard the restrained sob in his throat.

I swallowed hard, hands in fists, and waited for judgment.

"And if Troy wins?" It was Ares who asked, his head cocking

in a derisive sneer.

"If they win," I looked at him, looked at him with all the hatred I felt for him, "then you will leave me alone. You will release Hephaestus. All we have done will continue, and you will allow me to bring change to this mountain, as is the right of my creation as the Goddess of Beauty and Love."

Ares threw his head back with a humorless laugh.

But he looked at Zeus. For permission.

Zeus grinned. "Agreed. The wager stands."

"If Paris and Helen win, you leave us alone," I repeated. "If they lose, I submit to your ruling."

Zeus clapped. "It is done. Ares—"

But the God of War was on me already, glaring, his eyes bright with vehemence. "You do not know what you have done, Beauty," he told me. "A game that hinges on war? You arrange it for me, don't you?" He reached for me, but I wore my strophion; and so he recoiled with a sniff and rested the flat of his sword against his shoulder. "Now that I know my victory hangs on Troy's fall, I will set the full force of my power against that little city. You will be mine in days."

I held his gaze. Held even though I wanted to buckle. "We shall see," was all I could say without screaming.

He leaned close enough to sniff the air by my neck, and then he backed away, nodded at his demigods, and faced Zeus.

The soldiers threw Hephaestus to the ground. He toppled with a grunt and I spun on him, tears welling the moment I saw him—so much blood. Could a god lose this much and still mend? But already his skin was knitting together, so slowly though.

I knelt before him and touched his face, sweat-slicked and tear-stained, and his eyes met mine with a crash of force.

"What have you done?" he gasped. "Why did you—you should have let them punish me, Aphrodite—*why*—"

"Shh, it's all right," I told him, but it wasn't, none of this was all right. "Let's get you to the forge—I'll clean you—"

"For fairness," Zeus's voice boomed, "she'll be kept apart until the wager is concluded."

I froze, my hand on Hephaestus's cheek.

His eyes widened with panic. "Aphrodite—"

A net of gold—too familiar—draped over me.

Terror scoured me clean, but my body went immobile so I was emotion trapped in a reactionless cage. I fell, dragged backwards by Ares's soldiers. They weren't touching me themselves, and so the strophion was quiet and useless, and all my limbs were stiff in the net's enchantment. I couldn't even open my mouth to scream.

I helplessly watched Hephaestus panic.

"No—no, *wait*—" but he couldn't get to stand, his feet slipping on the blood-drenched floor as he held his mangled arm, pain lancing through him with a grimace and a snarl.

"Lock her in her suite," Zeus ordered, and Ares's soldiers dragged my stiff body through the crowd, leaving a trail of Hephaestus's blood as I swept through it.

A whimper vibrated in my chest, a subdued cry, a plea to stay, let me stay with him—

"*Wait!*" Hephaestus's shout banged off the banquet hall, but I lost sight of him in the press of the crowd.

Dozens of eyes stared down at me, an onslaught of—

Not of hunger.

Not of disdain.

Of . . . pity?

Of awe, maybe.

But I was gone, hauled away like cargo, listening to Hephaestus shout and beg for me to be brought back.

My eyes rolled shut and I steadied my breathing. I wasn't anywhere near the orb, but even so, I funneled what power I did when I was there—that Paris and Helen's love would endure. I had been enhancing their love nearly every day since my creation.

And now, I had to believe it would be strong enough to save us all.

26

Hephaestus

I had been here before. Ruined, aching, left to wallow in my own pain as the crowd dispersed, until only Zeus and Ares remained, looming over me.

My arm was only half-healed. The enchanted blade had cut deep. I had made it that way, to rend and slice even immortal flesh, just as I had made the gold net that had wrapped around her. This mountain was filled with my creations, and they had been my undoing.

Sweat poured down my face, my body twitching with the effort of my god-might healing my wound, and I looked up, glaring potent fury at Ares. And at Zeus. Let him see my rage; I was unmade now.

Zeus frowned at my anger. Did it give him pause? He sniffed and looked away. "Return to your forge, Hephaestus."

Ares whipped a startled look at him. "That is it? He will try to free her!"

"No. He won't. Will you?" Zeus looked down his nose at me. "You will honor this ruling, Hephaestus, or you will declare it forfeit."

"The same holds for him," I grunted with a nod at Ares, spittle flying, each word taking too much effort. The pain in my arm was dizzying, but I refused to pass out.

Zeus nodded. "You as well, Ares. Do not enter her suite, or forfeit."

Ares was silent a long moment. "Agreed."

Zeus sighed. It was the closest to true exasperation I had ever heard him. "I am tiring of this rivalry between you two. It will be good to have it settled."

"And his betrayal?" Ares stepped closer, eyeing my shoulder. "Is this punishment enough for turning against us?"

When Zeus did not immediately respond, both Ares and I looked at him, breaths holding.

The God-King stared up at the fake sky, hand stroking through his beard. "She said something interesting. That the right of her creation was to bring change to this mountain."

Ares flinched. "What? You take it seriously?"

But I managed to come to my feet, body shaking, eyelids fluttering as I fought to stay coherent. "It is her purpose, God-King," I said, every last remaining speck of my strength going to being reverent. "She can remake Olympus. We are long due for *new*, something truly new, aren't we? Let her bring it. Already she has brought so much—you have seen how the nymphs and demigods attend events now. How they walk more freely. That is her, these protections—"

"The enchanted items were her idea?"

Stupid. *Stupid.* My lips snapped shut. I was losing control of my mind, pain overwhelming my senses, so I could only stand there, dumb, and wilt.

Zeus nodded slowly. "Hm. There is much to be determined on this wager, then."

186

He said nothing else. No dismissal. He simply walked away, towards his arch, leaving me swaying on my feet, Ares fuming.

Ares spun on me. He had no pretense, either; he swung a fist into my gut that I couldn't counter in time, and I doubled forward with a wheezing gag.

"You will lose," he said to my bent form. "You will lose, and I make sure you know just how much you have truly lost every moment for the rest of our forever."

He marched away, and I wavered in stillness, in pain, alone, until his footsteps faded up the hall.

Then I turned and hobbled out, clutching my arm to my side, back down to my forge.

It felt so empty without her now. But I didn't let my mind linger; I tore through my supplies, gathering weapons I could strap with one hand. I twisted a bandage around my wound—the damn blood loss—and began the long, painful walk back up through the marble halls, to Aphrodite's suite.

No guards stood outside. As expected. Zeus relied on his word being threat enough, but I no longer would. And so I reached her door and sat heavily on the floor next to it, wincing as my body finally went slack.

Ares would not get to her. I would wait, here, until the war ended, until her wager completed. Would Zeus allow her to use the orb until then? I would, for her. I would pour all of my power into my mortals in Troy. But otherwise, I would be here, on the outside of her suite, listening for her, watching over her.

She was the bravest god I had ever seen. I was mute in awe of her, and as I sat in the silence of the empty hall, I closed my eyes, willing her to feel my presence outside her room.

Pain overcame me, welling high, pain and agony and fear

and disgust—
I would lose her if Troy fell.
Darkness closed in over me, and I was gone.

27

Aphrodite

Thalia, Aglaea, and Euphrosyne welcomed me back in somber grace.

I managed to tell them what had occurred, and they listened, their faces paling, only for Thalia to nod decisively when I sat in exhausted silence, done.

"Did Ares hurt you?" I asked her. My swollen eyes lifted to hers.

"Only to force the necklace on me," she said. But she looked away, and I wondered if she lied for my benefit; I reached for her hand, but she grasped mine quickly, squeezed tight.

"We will care for you, Goddess," she said. "To bed with you now."

But who cares for you? I wanted to ask.

I had tried to.

I had tried, and look where it had gotten us all.

Thalia pulled me into the bedchamber—my large, empty bedchamber, so bright and expansive compared to my home—and I laid there on the bed, curled in on myself, eyes slipping shut.

My fate, and the fate of Olympus, would be decided by love.

It was fitting.

It was terrifying.

My nymphs were free to walk the halls still, and so they brought me news of the war as the days progressed.

Greece seemed to be losing; Ares's shifting priorities had rattled the whole of the war, and so it appeared that the mighty Greeks were in retreat.

I sat at a chair by the sea window, sipping a steaming cup of tea, and did not react.

Greece left a parting gift, an offering for the gods they felt had abandoned them. Troy dragged it into their city and set it up as the center of their rejoicing over supposed victory.

Euphrosyne told me this, and tried to coax me to smile. "You have won, Goddess! Are you not happy?"

"Ares has not yet made his move," I said, my voice flat.

Thalia brushed my hair. I caught the way she eyed Euphrosyne and shook her head, and Euphrosyne bowed and slipped away.

"But Hephaestus sits outside your room still," Thalia told me. "He asks how you are."

My eyes slid to the wall beyond which I knew Hephaestus watched over me. I always touched the spot as I passed it, as though I could feel his warmth from beyond.

"Tell him," I started, my voice low, as though I was speaking just for him, "that I miss his bed." It was all I could allow myself to think of without falling apart.

"You will return to him soon," Thalia promised.

"What of Paris and Helen?" I asked with a throat clear, my eyes tearing.

Thalia set down the brush. "Together, in Troy's palace. They

190

do not rejoice as their city does."

"They are wise not to."

"You are morose, Goddess. This does mean victory, does it not? Perhaps love prevailed. Perhaps—"

There was a knock at the door.

Aglaea answered, keeping the door pulled so as not to show me within. She spoke quietly to whoever it was, and as I watched her, tension wound up my arms, knotted at the back of my neck.

But she twisted over her shoulder and beamed at me. "My lady, you have a gift."

"A gift?" I stood as Aglaea pulled the door open wide.

Immediately, my eyes leapt beyond, seeking Hephaestus. But he was not in view. I should not have wanted to see him, anyway; my nymphs had told me of Zeus's decree, that neither Ares nor Hephaestus were to intervene with me. How far did that stretch? I could not risk giving Ares reason to call the bet in his favor.

But there stood Hermes, the messenger god, the one who had summoned us from our forge, and for that my gut twisted with dislike of him.

Hermes bowed at the threshold. He held a basket laid with a cloth, and he set it at his feet before removing the cover. It showed a pile of fruit, sheened and vivid.

My brows furrowed and I eyed him as he straightened.

"For you, Goddess," he said, bowing again, though we were of the same rank.

"From—?"

"Me."

I stared at him. "I do not understand."

"I have not properly had chance to thank you." Hermes

tucked his hands behind his back. He was shorter than most gods, with a pale shock of light brown hair and wide eyes that made him look youthful.

"Thank me?"

"For . . ." He licked his lips, seeming to gather himself, and then nodded, deciding. "For the ring you gave to my beloved."

That drew me forward a step.

Hermes smiled, encouraging. "The ring has protected him in ways I could not. I did not even conceive of such a burden being lifted, but—thank you." His eyes pulled to the side, to where I knew Hephaestus stood in the hall. "Thank you both. For what it is worth, there are many here who are grateful as well, many among the gods."

He had begun to turn away when I finally found my voice.

"Other gods support these enchanted protections?" I asked.

Hermes looked over his shoulder with a toying grin. "Let's just say there has been a sudden renewed interest in supporting Troy in this war."

But still, the knowledge of Troy's *win* felt . . . wrong. I could not place it.

"You are welcome," I told him, eyes tearing, and Hermes bowed again, and left.

Aglaea left the door open for a beat, sneaking me a sly grin, but Hephaestus did not step into view. I felt the weight of his presence, so near, and it maddened me that I could not run into his arms.

We had brought a right change to Olympus. A change even other gods were in support of.

That buoyed me more than Greece's retreat, and as Aglaea shut the door, I smiled.

Others heard of Hermes's gift, and more followed suit.

Baskets and packages and letters. Outpourings from nymphs and demigods, and a few other gods as well—all thanking me for what I had done in creating these protective items. My rooms filled with proof of the goodness I had helped blossom.

I pressed my hand to the spot on the wall, grinning, wanting so badly to see his face. The guests thanked Hephaestus too; they *thanked* him, acknowledged his skill, finally, *finally* giving him the credit he had so long been denied.

This felt like victory.

And so I began to believe in Troy's success. In Greece's retreat. In Paris and Helen's survival and enduring love.

Any day now, Zeus would declare the war ended, and I would return home.

So when Hermes again came, and Aglaea opened the door for him, I expected to see him grinning.

But his eyes were bloodshot. He stayed still on the threshold, speaking to me and half-speaking to Hephaestus as well.

"The offering the Greeks left was a trap," he said. "A small militia was hidden within. They waited for the Trojans to get drunk on celebration, then they slipped out, opened the gates of the city, and allowed the whole of the Greek army within. The city has been razed."

Oh, this was the trick I had suspected of Ares, a brutal switch of war, and as Hermes spoke, I sank to a chair, shock rending me nearly limp.

"What of Paris and Helen?" I barely heard my own question.

Thalia eyed me strangely. She was weeping. "My lady? Did you not hear—"

But Hermes shook his head. "They escaped, along with a few of the Trojan royals. But the war is declared. Greece is the victor."

They escaped.

Paris and Helen were alive.

My hand rose to my lips, and Aglaea fell upon me, thinking my reaction sorrow. It wasn't—it was tangled and heady and a dozen things, but not sorrow.

I rose from the chair. "I will see Zeus now."

Hermes nodded. "He waits for you. Goddess—" He took a steadying breath. "I am sorry."

I stepped forward, crossing the room, the hem of my gold gown dragging behind me. And when I smiled at him, I know it shocked him; he flinched, uncertain why I would be happy.

"Thank you," I told him.

He bowed away, giving me space to leave. But before I followed him, I turned to Thalia.

"Hephaestus is outside still?"

Hermes was the one who said, "Yes, Goddess."

I saw a shadow move. I recognized its shape, would know it anywhere.

"Please wait for me in the banquet hall," I told him. "Please."

We were so close.

So very close.

I could not risk this wager on our nearness now, on seeing him or him seeing me before Zeus officially called it.

The request did not break me as I thought it would. I was stone now, calm in a way that I had not been in all my time here.

I knew my purpose. Fully.

And I would not fail it.

The shadow moved away. As it did, I wanted to cry out for him; but Hermes nodded when Hephaestus was gone.

Hands in fists, I took a step.

"My lady," Thalia said. "Your strophion!"

My jaw set. I eyed it in her hands.

"No, thank you, Thalia." I smiled at her. "I will not need it."

Her face went white. She feared for me. I should have as well, perhaps, but my centered calmness carried me out of my suite for the first time in days—weeks? Time had lost meaning, had never had it at all.

My nymphs were around me, Hermes leading us up through Olympus.

As we walked, the rooms we passed were empty. None of the usual parties or bored relaxation. Had the war drawn all focus? Had—

My wondering cut off when I entered the banquet hall.

And there, I saw the whole of Olympus now, truly, not merely the same cluster of gods I had come to expect. But *everyone*—all nymphs, all demigods, all who were not immortal. They pressed in this space more numerous than the gods, and when I appeared, they all came to attention.

There was no hunger in these eyes. No possession.

They looked at me, and I felt only love.

These were the lives we had changed with our protective enchantments. This was the heart of Olympus, born anew in the potential of a changed future.

The crowd parted, leading a path once again to Zeus's throne. At its base waited Ares, and—

I stumbled faster, catching myself, my composure, when I saw Hephaestus.

I wanted to run to him. To fling myself into his arms and weep and kiss those lips. My mind and body had fallen into a sort of numb survival state without him, but now that I saw him, I felt how very long it had been since I had laid eyes on him. His wound was healed, his shoulder whole, but he looked gaunt and gray, his face sunken in barely repressed terror.

The whole of the room bore that same pause of fear. That Greece had won. That the wager was lost.

They had not realized.

They did not know.

I stopped before Zeus, hands knotted behind my back.

Ares, immediately, approached me.

I let him grab my arm.

"Victory is mine, Beauty," he said down to me. He was in his war garb still, blood smeared from Troy's fall, and he wreaked of sweat and smoke. "I will have that victory now."

He stepped past me, dragging me with him, and I knew what he meant—a consummation, the one he had envisioned since Peleus and Thetis's wedding.

I did not budge. My eyes lifted to Zeus's. "Ares did not win me," I said in a clear, snapping voice.

Ares shot a look down at me. "Do not try to get out of this. The wager said—"

"That if Paris and Helen lost, you would have me." I glared up at him, my lips unable to suppress a slight grin. "But Paris and Helen won."

"Did you not hear? Troy fell. I saw it burn." Ares's grip pinched tighter, painful, bruising. "Accept it, Beauty. It will be easier."

"But *Paris and Helen* escaped Troy, didn't they? They escaped with their love intact." Again, I directed the words at Zeus, who sat on his throne, hand on his chin, eyes narrow. "That was my wager. Paris and Helen. I never mentioned Troy."

Hephaestus sipped in a breath and rose straighter. I could

not look at him, but I felt the difference in his posture. Hope. He saw now what I had done.

All of the room did.

Gasps went around. A cheer shot up, silenced quickly.

All held, watching Zeus.

Who stared at me. Weighing my words. The wager made. Ares's growing rage.

Finally, Zeus threw his head back, clapped his hands together, and laughed.

"Oh, she *is* clever, isn't she? Goddess of cunning!" He rose from his throne with another rolling laugh. "Release her, Ares. You have lost."

My chest bucked, a rising spurt of joy, and alongside it, the room erupted.

Cheers. Applause. Nymphs and demigods and more. All cheering. *For me.*

Ares whirled on Zeus. "You—*you cannot do this.* Troy fell! That was—"

"That was not the wager made," Zeus said with a chuckle. "Oh, even I admit to missing that! But her wording was clear. Hephaestus," he waved at me, "collect your bride."

I finally looked at him.

The relief on Hephaestus's face was palpable and beautiful, as brilliant as the sun. He needed no further prodding, and neither did I.

I dove forward, but Ares had not released my arm, and he jerked me back as I moved.

Hephaestus's relief snapped into rage. "Ares, *release her*—"

But I let the momentum of the swing yank me back, closer to Ares.

I was ready for him now.

I slammed my knee up into his crotch with a nauseating crunch.

Ares buckled instantly. He dropped his grip on me, and that was all the victory over him I needed—I never would think on him again.

The crowd, though, roared, laughter and further cheering, something in them had been unleashed at my victory and Ares's loss. Too many had lived in fear under the rules he had lived by.

I spun back and Hephaestus was there. He was there, and he was weeping, and I hurled my body into his arms, my own tears falling. Relief and joy unleashed through me in a rapid chaos, and I did not fully feel the brunt of what I had won until Hephaestus was in my arms, his solidness beneath me, his lips on my neck.

Paris and Helen's love had endured. The gift I had given them, the blessing of a goddess, had survived a war and the interference of gods and it had saved everything I held most precious. And all around me were the rejoicing cries of those I had helped, lives that I had begun to change.

I had wondered once what good love and beauty could bring to a mountain of corruption.

Now I knew.

I knew, and I wept in that beautiful knowledge as I held my love.

28

Hephaestus

I did not know how to process the noise that filled the banquet hall.

It was *joyous*. Joyous, where this mountain only ever heard sighs of boredom or muffled screams. There was no joy here, not in Olympus, no reason to cheer.

Until now.

Until her.

My wife.

Now and forever, unable to be stolen by Ares, confirmed twice over by Zeus—it was done, done before all of Olympus, and by the cheers that came, I knew we were safer in our victory than any had ever been.

Ares drew up from where her hit to his groin had left him. He did not look at us, not even to give a threatening scowl, and that retreat set my heart soaring. There was no fight in him now, not as he sulked through the crowd that cried out for us.

We had won. Because of my ingenious, determined wife, because of this Goddess of Beauty and Love who, remarkably, poured that love onto me.

Aphrodite still in my arms, I twisted to look up at Zeus.

He surveyed the crowd with a spark of interest.

"She is that good change," I told him, shouting over the crowd.

Zeus snapped his eyes to me. There was a beat where I saw his offense still that I had made these items without his approval, a beat further of him considering what sort of threat I was.

But I had my wife back in my arms. I was no threat to anyone now.

He nodded. "It would seem so. Change in Olympus." His eyes slid to Aphrodite, who kept her face buried in my shoulder. "Beautiful change."

He stepped down from his throne and vanished into the crowd. How would he allow Olympus to shift after this day? I did not know.

But we would be there to see it, and to guide it towards a better future.

Music began to play, and another cheer went up as the pop of a wine cask opened.

"A party," she said into me. I felt the words more than heard them. "For us?"

"It would seem so." I set her down, keeping my arms around her waist, her body not nearly close enough to mine. But I needed my lips on hers, and as I kissed her, she arched up into it, mouth opening for me in perfect eagerness.

"Should we stay for it?" she asked.

I did want to see what sort of affair this would be. It would not devolve into a dangerous chase through Olympus's halls or an orgy of strain and fear.

But Aphrodite nipped at my mouth. Licked along the ridge

of my lips as I smiled.

"It will last for hours likely," I told her.

She lifted onto her toes and said into my ear, "So will I. Can you, husband?"

The crash of joy and relief erupted in me, unleashing a wave of repressed desire that hit upon me tenfold. I hefted her into my arms and her legs wrapped around my hips and a whoop echoed through the crowd, but we were beyond caring; our kisses deepened, ravenous, it had been far, far too long since I had tasted her and felt her warmth.

They cheered her as we left. "Aphrodite! Aphrodite!"

And then, "Hephaestus!"

That had me flinching, instinct telling me it was in threat or warning—but the voices were pure with adoration.

Aphrodite smiled against me. "They will see you as I see you now," she told me.

Once, I had wanted that. To be no longer a recluse. To walk the halls of Olympus and feel welcome. It had become such a far-off dream that I had not truly wanted it in decades, but now, she made all of it real. Not everything would change immediately—no doubt Ares and Apollo and those likes would rail against these greater freedoms and more determined boundaries—but the party filling the banquet hall we left behind was testament to everything this goddess had brought to me, impossible dreams coming true.

I could not get her to our forge fast enough. Could not stop kissing her, feeling a repeat of our wedding day, and by the time I shut the door behind us, she was biting my lip and moaning my name in such a breathy, needy whine that I did not even make it to our bed—I dumped her on a worktable.

"I will make a feast of your body, Goddess," I told her, ripping the gown off her shoulders. "Every part of you—I must taste it all again—"

She gasped, drawing back suddenly, and there was a spark of realization in her eyes. I recognized it: an idea forming.

"Aphrodite," I growled, "if you have thought of a project to do, as the God of Craftsmanship, I *demand* it be completed *far later*—"

She giggled. It was such a girlish, innocent noise to come from her that my half-hard cock went fully erect and I pressed my mouth to her neck, beginning my feast there.

"No, no, not a project! Not like *that*—Hephaestus! Wait—" She wiggled against the table until I backed up.

And then, before my eyes, the Goddess of Beauty dropped to her knees in front of me.

The way she looked up at me.

The beat of her eyelashes on her cheeks. The catch of her lower lip between her teeth.

I rocked forward, bracing myself on the table, caging her body beneath mine. "Aphrodite. What are you doing?"

"Feasting, husband." She grabbed the band of my kilt and pulled, hard, her thin fingers expertly yanking the whole of the material over my thighs and down until it puddled at the floor around my feet.

My cock lifted free, the tip red and glistening, and my breath knotted in my chest. In all our lovemaking, she had not yet taken me in her mouth, and that absence rebounded through me now. I had been so utterly obsessed with her cunt that I had not realized how delectable that mouth looked until she held my gaze and leaned in.

Her soft pink lips parted, that little tongue darting out to lick the tip of my cock, and it bobbed at the contact, my whole body seizing with a wave of desire.

She *moaned*. And giggled again. And I bit down into my arm to keep from coming.

"I wanted to do that the moment I first saw you naked," she said. Her hand lifted and she grabbed the base of me, holding it steady before her face.

If it had looked large when aimed at her small cunt, it looked even more massive now as she knelt on the floor of my forge, her gown streaked at the knees with soot. This exquisite creature should not be on the floor among such filth, but her eyes met mine, and she must have seen the thought on my face.

"I am yours, Hephaestus," she promised and licked the tip again, taking it between her lips in one gentle suck. "I am yours." Another, deeper, this goddess was pushing her delicate mouth down around my cock while she knelt on the floor of my forge, and my body shuddered, my mind unable to comprehend the improbable, incredible, *inconceivable* events that had led to this moment of delirious rapture.

"Mine," I ground out, slowly losing control.

She moaned her assent, the vibrations vaulting up my cock, and she began to thrust, taking me deep into her mouth until the tip slammed up against the wall of her throat. The contact had my hips bucking, and she moaned again, shifting for a better angle, bobbing her head in rhythmic pulses as her tongue lapped around my shaft, up into my slit—

I bellowed out, holding down my release only by the sheer threads of effort, and I grabbed beneath her arms and hoisted her up and threw her back onto the table. She protested, her lips glossy and plump, but I kissed away her words, scrambling to disrobe her fully.

As I trailed my lips down her neck, she went silent, relenting to my work. Yes, yes, I was the God of Skill, and she was my utmost project, my masterpiece, and I committed myself to her study in all ways as I drew her nipple between my lips and suckled, hard, flicking the tip with my tongue.

Her careening mewl was a symphony, and I would hear its crescendo. I yanked her ass to hang over the table's edge and on her startled gasp I sheathed myself in her, rocking so off balance that we both landed out flat on the table, our bodies shuddering in tandem at the devastating intimacy of being united again.

"Hephaestus." Her voice pinched, tears brimming, and I began to thrust, snaking one hand between us to draw languid circles around her clit.

"Aphrodite," I whispered into her hair. The smell of her infused me, pricked tears in my eyes—I had feared I would never again be here, that I would have to exist without her, and so to have her back, to once again have our bodies writhing into each other—

She came first. She always would. I felt her clit swell beneath my thumb and she threw her head back and whimpered more than screamed, but I understood—she was crying. I was too, tears mingling with sweat as I fell apart inside of her.

"Kiss me," she begged, and I obeyed, our bodies still joined, the light of the forge casting us in orange and gold.

"You are home," I growled into her mouth. I was angry, angry at the fear ebbing in my chest; angry at the moments we had missed; angry that we had forever now, and it was still not enough. "You are home, and you are mine."

"Yes, Hephaestus—"

"Say it."

Her lips curled into a smile against mine. "I love when you

do that. I never told you."

I smiled back, my fingers clamping on her thigh, yanking her against me as my cock grew stiff again, right in her softening cunt. "Say it, Goddess."

"I am home," she said it as a moan, the way she knew drove me wild, all desperate breath. "I am yours." Her ankles locked around my back, digging into my ribcage, and she lay out on the table, spread her arms over her head and displayed herself for me in the forge light.

"Now, husband." She grinned, sultry, teasing. "Show me how much I belong to you."

29

Aphrodite

I awakened in our bed, my head on Hephaestus's chest, though I had no memory of ending up there. Snatches of it came to me—I winced, knowing we had utterly destroyed the worktables, but I could not stop the slow crawl of my smile at how perfect that destruction had been.

I lifted my chin to see his eyes shut, his breathing low and even. A beat after I moved, though, he stirred, until his long lashes flickered apart, and his eyes met mine.

We held there, watching each other, for minutes that stretched into hours, because we had that time now.

I danced my fingers across his wide chest, playing through his dark, tangled hair. "Do you think the party is still going?"

He groaned deep in his throat and tightened his arm against my naked body. "I don't care in the least."

"We should." I eyed him with a new light. "We no longer have to hide here."

He winced, but managed a half sincere smile. "That should change, shouldn't it? We must become more a part of this mountain, actively."

I climbed up over him, settling my hips across the hill of his. His soft cock sat beneath my equally softened and thoroughly drenched cunt, still sensitive and pliant from our lovemaking.

"I do not want to share you with everyone just yet," I admitted.

He dug his fingers into the cushions of my hips. "I was thinking the same thing."

"Oh?" I bent forward to lightly trace my lips across his. "I wonder if we have the same other thought."

"Hm?"

"I was thinking," I rocked my hips and pulled back to prop over him, breasts swinging, "about what our next project should be."

That set something in his eyes, and he looked up at me, his head tipping on the bedding.

The smile he gave was the epitome of happiness, the very pinnacle of beauty, from the sparkle in his eye to the swell of his cheeks over his beard.

Our lifetime spread out before me. Giving beauty and love to mortals. Continuing to strengthen the beauty and love in Olympus, now by showing them what joy could be found in love rather than competition and cruelty.

Continuation, and joy, and steadiness, and at the crux of it all, him.

I kissed him again, something hot twisting deep beneath my belly button. I would never tire of his mouth, not now, not in a millennia.

He spun us, pinning me beneath him as the light catcher sent out glitter showers of teal and blue, and he ran his hand up the rise of my leg, brushed his lips over my ear.

"The God of Craftsmanship is yours to use, Goddess," he

promised me. "What beautiful thing should we make next?"

About the Author

Natasha Luxe is the pseudonym of a bestselling author living in the Midwest. She writes romance such as the Heroes and Villains series with Liza Penn as well as her solo books, the Celebrity Crush series and the Club Reverie series.

You can connect with me on:
🌐 https://www.thepennandluxe.com

Subscribe to my newsletter:
✉ https://rarebooks.substack.com/welcome

Also by Natasha Luxe

MEET CUTE
Free NOW on Kindle Unlimited

I do not have time for distractions... like global heartthrob Tom Hudel, who comes to my island to film his new movie.

No matter how melting his smile is. No matter how dizzying his accent is. No matter how gentle his eyes are. I will not get distracted by a celebrity crush.

PLOT TWIST
Free NOW on Kindle Unlimited

I've learned my lesson when it comes to dating actors... Until I start on the set of a movie featuring the newest hot shot leading man, Sebastian Stanik. He awakens parts of me I'd thought were long gone.

Maybe a little fun won't kill me, but the moment this movie wraps, the barriers are going back up. I will not fall for a celebrity crush.

OFF CAMERA
Free NOW on Kindle Unlimited

Interning for a Hollywood PR agency is a dream job—so when they ask me to faux-date LA bad boy Chris Griffins, I agree. The only problem is, he's a way better actor than I expected...unless all those sidelong glances and electric touches mean he really is into me?

Even crazier...am I actually into him?

I cannot have real feelings for a celebrity crush.

FAE PRINCE
Free NOW on Kindle Unlimited

Sloane is in love with the dark and intense Fae Prince Kilian. Or at least, she pretends to be, using what few free hours she has to get lost in the series of sultry books about him.

Until she hears about a new club that promises to take her wildest fantasies and make them a reality.

She knows this is a virtually created world. Isn't it?

VILLAIN GOD
Free NOW on Kindle Unlimited

Devyn has created the perfect virtual replica of her favorite sci-fi world — complete with that world's villain, the immortal god Nazar.

She has spent her whole life studying the boundaries between fantasy and reality...but for Nazar, she might just break those boundaries entirely.

CPSIA information can be obtained
at www.ICGtesting.com
Printed in the USA
BVHW050353130223
658293BV00015B/1843

9 798218 019990